SOMHAIRLE UÍ DHÚGÁIN

A TITHE OF BLOOD

To Maddy. For always pushing me to write <3

Happy Valentine's Day

2

Chapter 1

Wind blew west from the frozen peaks mountains past the frigid shores of a distant land, picking up speed as it battered the wooden homes dotting the coast, the thick linens battering on the clothesline from where they hung, strung between the small cottages. The wind climbed in speed as it crossed the Tempest Sea, aptly named by the locals for its ever present storms, thundering waves rising, attempting to push back at the gusts. On and on the winds blew until they came to the Darkwood forest plunging between the damp twisted trees, shaking off the leaves early to change with the coming of autumn. One of these leaves lazily rode the now gentle breeze through the still shaking branches and onto the wide expanse of broad, tall grasses that coated the plain like a shagged carpet of green and gold, and within this sea of grass, moving slowly, a small band of youths stalked their prey.

Alix followed the Longhorn through the tall grass of the vast meadow that made up her world. Moving the stiff grasses gently to the side as her group began to spread out around their prey. Alix moved an errant blade out of her way, preventing it from catching on her thick linen skirt, now hiked up and tied between her legs. The minute seeds of the grass, looked like small grains of sand, each forming a small divot in the fibrous stalk. They provided a rhythmic *shuck* as the wind swept over her, she matched her movements as best she could with the sound. She could see the longhorn and did not want to send yet another easy kill to escape her again. She still had not heard the end of the teasing from the older boys.

The longhorn's head rose from where it was chewing seeds off the stalk. Its head swinging to scan the horizon, the long intimidating almost black horn sprouting almost three feet from its long fur covered head. It stamped one of its powerful long legs and let out a long puff before lowering its head to return to lazily chew at the grass again. Alix moved a hand up to brush a strand of tightly curled auburn hair from her eyes, a feature that all her clann shared. She gently placed her hunting pack on the ground, her eyes never leaving the longhorn. She pulled her bow off her back and nocked an arrow, the head of which was narrow and long, it needed to be to do its job correctly, Longhorns were notoriously hard to kill unless done correctly.

Its brown shaggy hair moved with the wind and Alix pulled back the waxed string of her bow tight, the bow, curved and made from the horn of past kills, flexed with her and she waited. The wind died down and she let her arrow fly. Her aim was true and the arrow wedged itself deep in the side of the beast. It rose on its back legs, attempting a howl, but Alix's aim had been sound and the beast struggled to cry out before it fell to the ground. It let out a shuddering breath then silence, its brown fur now stained red.

"Great shot!", came a shout, Alix turned as one of her kin rose from the grass.

"I still don't know how you do it" chuckled Jason, the eldest living of her many cousins. His hair was a match of hers in curls, though his hair was dark enough that the red seemed almost a deep brown until it caught the light. It bounced around as he bounded over to join Alix as she admired her kill laughing as the rest of the group bounded from their hiding spots to join them.

"Alright boys, let's get started". He hollered, smacking Alix on the back as the two other boys jumped to join him. First was Rick, small but wiry, his ginger hair trimmed short to his scalp. Shay followed behind. He was the tallest of the bunch, his hair a match of Jason's though his face which now showed no few whiskers which he claimed to be a beard. They were cousins in the same way all of the clann Muintir were. Related somehow through blood, though the lines were long and mixed and oftentimes confusing. Alix followed the boys as they quickly began prepping the longhorn for travel, using large bronze knives to hack away at the six large legs of the longhorn, working to separate them to allow for travel, leaving the rest of the carcass for whatever came after him.

"Alix keep a lookout, yeah?" asked Jason, though it was not needed, Alix was already scanning the horizon, on the lookout for the creatures that would be drawn to a kill of this size. Longhorns were nowhere near a rare sight this side of the peaks, but there was little that could truly threaten one. A dead Longhorn would have any local wildlife in the area racing for a mouthful before it was all gone. Already she could see the four winged silhouette of a plain's vulture begin to circle above. The vulture would not attack them, they were more opportunistic scavengers than dangerous predators, but it was a sign their kill was not going to stay a secret much longer.

Looking north, towards the peaks, the Domain of the gods, curse their names and a blight on their home, she scanned the deepwood that began to dominate the lands before the mountain, just visible on the horizon. It marked the boundary of her clann, sacred stones with wards against spirits, preventing them from accessing the land of the living. She couldn't see anything from this distance of several miles, but fear of the forest and the mountains beyond, demanded she be vigilant.

A movement in the grassland, a few hundred feet away caught her attention. There the stalks of grass still swayed, but

6

out of step with those around them. She hefted her bow, holding it in a low tight grip, an arrow nocked but not drawn. Out of the corner of her eye, she saw Shay's head raise from his work before turning back to the carcass, he and her cousins working faster and harder to separate as much of the meat and skin from the carcass as they could. The thing moving through the grasses continued to approach and Alix took the time to steady herself, planting her feet. The shape was too low to the ground to be an Erlking. It was too late in the summer to be a Taeris. She continued to scan the horizon and once the disturbance was only a few dozen feet away she let out a single whistle and the boys expertly, with well practised hands, grabbed their tools and baskets in which they had placed the harvested meat and moved quickly away from the carcass.

Alix followed. She scooped up her pack, quickly slinging it onto her back before slowly moving backwards, bow still at the ready as she moved away from the bloody remains of the Longhorn. With one last glance at what remained of the Longhorn and turned to jog after her quickly retreating cousins. She turned for one last glance before *What is it?* She wondered again, though luckily she didn't need to wonder long as from the grass two powerful shoulders pulled themselves into the clearing.

The Great Wolf's amber eyes fixed on her. Sitting above a mouth of razor-sharp teeth, the sharp snout of the wolf stood level with her head. It paused and she could see the huge musculature of the beast hidden beneath its thick curls of pitch black hair. The two small horns behind its short and pointed ears seemed to darken as it maintained eye contact, dark magik building within the powerful monster. She could see the hair on its back behind grow as its shoulders seemed to elongate as the

Great Wolf pulled itself up out of its crouch. Showing her it's full size, standing close to ten feet. It was said the look of the Great Wolf was death and as she looked into those amber gold eyes she felt her hands begin to shake, the bow dipping towards the ground as she felt dread and fear rise throughout her body. The Great Wolf cocked its head at her before releasing a growl that shook her bones before turning from her towards the longhorn.

Alix, released from the Great Wolf's gaze, turned and ran, catching up with her cousins as they continued their canter through the grass back home. The great wolves were said to be of the old magik, the dark arts of the gods, bringing pain and destruction to the world of the living. She reached them before they had crested the opposing hill, turning in the hollow to follow the divide towards the coast.

"Did you see that?" she exclaimed. She must have been slightly out of breath at the hard pace as even to her, her usually monotone voice sounded shrill.

"It was a Great Wolf!" This caused Jason to stumble and Shay and Rick stopped in their tracks to turn to her.

"A Great Wolf?" started Rick almost at the exact time Shay asked, "Did it tell you your death?"

"Stop it boys," Jason interrupted before Alix could respond.

"Great Wolves almost never come down to the grasses, everyone knows that. It was probably an Erlking". Jason did not spend much of his time out in the grass and appeared to not know that it was too late in the season for Erklings. Alix opened her mouth to say just so but a howl that seemed to shake the ground erupted from the direction of the longhorn's carcass. Rick fell to the ground, dropping his basket. Alix and the rest stood still, their eyes wide as they watched to see if the Great Wolf would emerge.

After a long pause, the Howl came again and as one they spun and began to sprint back, any sense of pacing themselves long forgotten.

"What was that?" Jason exclaimed,

"Let's not waste time here!" Rick responded and for the first time, she saw fear in her cousin's eyes. Finding words were failing her she nodded and followed as Jason turned the group and took off. Slower than before. Shay, normally one who seemed never able to be quiet, followed silently along at the back, his usual tan skin now a more sickly hue. They finished the last few miles home in terrified and confused silence.

***

The sun was high in the sky as the group finally trampled up the hill to their village. As they arrived, noisily collapsing in the village centre, the commotion brought people out from their cottages and in from the fields to come see the young group's recent haul. Keemre led the procession of happy faces who came to greet the panting and sweaty youths and her apprentices followed behind, moving to take the baskets from the boys, passing out water skins which the boys drank quickly from. Keemre, the village chief handed a full water skin to Alix and with a smile as she embraced Alix.

"Good work, child". She said softly.

Despite their run in with the terrifying beast, the hugs and laughter from their family at the successful hunt brought had them all smiling and laughing in return. Music quickly started up from a drum from ole man Red's hut as the gap-toothed man smiled out at the crowd. A flute and pipes joined Red's drum almost immediately, and soon the village was alive with music as the villagers busied themselves with unburdening the hunting group of their load and prepping the meat for salting. A successful hunt meant a feast, but a feast meant hours of work. Few, except Alix and her cousins, would be spared from being put to work today. But by the end of tonight, most of the casks of wine would be tapped and no one would be complaining. Least of all Alix who had finally become old enough to sit with the adults and take part in the wine. She of course was no stranger to the strong wine, but drinking it with her cousins openly was very different than drinking late at night in the dark outside the walls.

Alix finished the waterskin and handed it back to Keemre who was now inspecting the bow.

"How was it, child?" She asked, turning the bow over in her hand before handing it back to Alix, who stood.

"The hunt went fine, but Keemre, I saw another one". Keemre stepped closer, taking Alix by the hand. Her eyes scanned Alix's face, her eyes now serious.

"Come with me, child". She said as she led Alix through the crowd now busy and noisy with work and past them to the village hall, and as clann chief, Keemre's home. Alix looked back once before stepping into the large building. Jason and Shay had been quickly approached by their parents who hugged them close as Jason was loudly describing the adventure, barely audible over the music. Rick, was being held by his mother while his older sister punched him playfully.

Keemre grabbed a pillow and sat down on the raised dias in the centre of the large main room, inviting Alix to join her, grabbing a matching pillow. Normally no one would sit with the clann chief like this but, Alix was Keemre's favourite, especially since the death of her parents, and was apparently entitled to bend some of the rules.

She had come to be Keemre's ward after her mother had passed during childbirth, her unborn brother dying with her. Keemre had been forced to explain to the child Alix what had happened, that her brother's soul had accompanied her mother's soul to the great beyond to keep her safe, though now approaching her twentieth year, Alix knew that was only a story you told a child too distraught by the loss of her family to eat. She had spent twelve years in Keemre's home, learning the history of her clann alongside her cousins during the mornings, spending her evenings stalking the grassland and running wild through the tall grasses in search of mythical beasts to hunt.

It was said some beings of magik still roamed the world and if you could catch one they would perform miracles for you, she had always hoped to catch one, to wish it to return her mother and brother to her. After being caught sneaking out yet again, Keemre had decided to teach her how to hunt safely.

"If you are to sneak out, let us teach you enough not to trip and fall into an Erkling's mouth". She had said. It had turned out that Keemre was not just a good hunter, she was likely the best on the whole plain. At the annual games, she could still shoot the bow farther than any other archer that entered. Even those from Clann Arcus who were famed for their archery.

So as Alix's skill had grown, she moved into the role of game hunter. Keemre loved to hunt though she was now far too old to go out onto the plains by herself. So instead, she would have Alix tell her of the hunt. And Alix had learnt over time to be as detailed as possible, the weather, the birds and beasts she saw, all of which Keemre claimed she was able to read as omens. Though secretly, Alix thought she was just reliving her youth through these stories.

"So, tell me of your hunt, Alix". Keemre said eagerly lounging back against a pillow and rug made from longhorn fur. She rested her head against its mixed red and black fur as she took a swig of wine from a carved mug at her side. So, as with every time before, Alix regaled the wise woman clann chief with the story of the hunt. Keemre reclined on her pillow and interrupted with questions as Alix spoke, asking the shade of the foliage, time of day of events, and anything that could add, as Keemre always asked for "more colour" in her stories but, as she got to the part with the Great Wolf, her demeanour changed. She sat forward and listened intently. Not asking any questions until the end.

"You heard a roar?" she asked.

"Yes, it threw us to the ground, as if a gust had swept us away" replied Alix.

"That is a powerful omen, Alix, and not a good one at that". Keemre was very serious now, a mood that Alix rarely saw her in. Alix blinked and swallowed the stone that had appeared in her throat. Keemre looked at her a moment before humming a single dull note, a habit of hers when worried.

"I don't like that Child, The clann must be on watch tonight, I will speak to my sisters and do the necessary rituals, but if there is a Great Wolf in the grasses. I don't want it to have found a way back here".

"Do you think it did?" Alix asked, now worried. "Followed us I mean", she added.

"Unlikely, Great Wolves are of the Darkforest; they rarely venture too close to the coast, it is said they hate the grasses but, all the same, it is a beast of Magik, we cannot easily kill it or scare it off. Best to be safe and watchful". With that Keemre rose, likely to relay her decision to her apprentices.

"Do not worry child, they hate humans, especially groups of us together, we will be safe". She said with a smile Alix could tell was forced. And with that, she turned and walked out into the sun waving down the younger of her apprentices, who was giggling and twirling her hair while standing over Ric who was busy using his knife to cut up the Monohorn meat for roasting.

Alix rose and moved to follow, keen to get to her chores and her own bed. She was a hunter, one of the few jobs in the clann that allowed her to avoid most of the basic daily tasks that kept the clann working and the village clean and in good repair but, she also had her own small hut to deal with, which meant sweeping out the dust, stoking the heart and gathering kindling and firewood from the nearby copses, which still took up most of an afternoon. But, as she neared the door a twinkle out of the corner of her eye caught her attention.

The beast's long narrow horn was in a small basin of water. It was to be boiled and flattened, likely to make jewellery, or other fine gifts by the apprentices, for Alix to keep or give out come the next festival day. Keemre was eager for her to attract a man and hoped each time she returned with a beast, she would use the jewellery as a betrothal gift, each time quietly disappointed as she handed out the tokens to her cousins.

The dark blue of the horn glistened as it caught the light of the sun, glittering like sunlight on the water. Something, however, seemed off, weird. Alix leaned closer wondering if the Monohorn had some oddity to it, *a disease perhaps?* when

13

a deep blue fire seemed to run within the grooves of the horn, the odd blue flame seemed to give off no heat but an odd glow that seemed to suck in the light, not give any off. It seemed dangerous, but she could not look away.

Alix, transfixed by the dark flames, did not realise her hand had moved to grab the horn until Keemre's sinewy arm, still strong from the labours of living on the grassland, snatched her hand away. But still, the horn held her attention, it seemed to call her to it,

"It's alright child", Keemre was saying as she slowly but firmly pulled Alix away, her eyes not rising from the still burning horn. Two apprentices rushed into the room, both stood stunned as they spied the horn, burning an odd shade of blue before Keemre snapped at them, her voice harsh. "Quickly, girls". She said as they jumped into action. One moved to grab a blanket from a basket set by the dias, the other pulled shut the curtain doors to the room, they covered the horn with the blanket and suddenly, the room seemed to brighten as the horn's odd light was extinguished. Keemre pulled the blanket off the horn and suddenly the burning deep blue horn had reverted back to, well a horn.

Alix, now finding her words said, "What was that?" she asked the question between increasingly deeper breaths. Keemre did not answer, instead turning to her apprentices and barking out orders. "Bury that blanket with whistle weed and tornwood. Then, light three of the tallow candles and place them around this house". The apprentices didn't wait for further context and jumped to obey, clearly they knew more of what was going on. Alix made a sound that was meant to be a word, but one look from Keemre silenced her. Only once both apprentices had gone, with Alix's formerly burning horn in tow, did Keemre turn to address her.

"You are lucky to be alive, girl". She said as Alix flinched at the words, Keemre only used girl when she was truly close to exploding. "What was that?" Alix asked again, decidedly more calm than she felt. Keemre adjusted her robe before shrugging, showing a level of frustration and annoyance that scared Alix. This had shaken the wise woman.

"I don't know. Magik to be sure, but I have never seen anything like that before". They sat in the uncomfortable silence a moment longer before Keemre moved to Alix's side, pulling her into a tight embrace.

"Don't scare me like that again, Child". She said and Alix hugged her back. The image of the burning horn still shone bright in her mind, the fear and dread clear on Keemre's face scaring her in a way she had never felt before.

"I won't," she said.

Chapter 2

The next few days passed in relative peace, the feast had taken place as expected, and though all talk around the large fire the villagers had erected was about the hunt and, more specifically, the young group's run-in with the Great Wolf, Alix had claimed to feel exhausted from the prolonged days spent out in the grasses, and retired early most nights, keen to catch up on sleep.

There was no mention of the horn or the odd flame again, at least not to Alix or anywhere she might have overheard. Keemre's apprentices shared their master's tendency for tight lips, for which she was grateful, but truly, Alix was exhausted. She had spent the last few nights tossing and turning in her bed, the experience with the horn had seemed to have drained her and unfortunately, robbed her of the freedom of restful sleep, free from dreams of the most terrifying kind. Her dreams had been nothing but Alix being chased by some giant Wolf beast, her friends and family roasted on spits as she screamed for help.

On the fourth day back, Keemre, recently returned from a visit to a nearby village of clann Lairge to trade some of the dried Longhorn meat, called her to the big house. Alix dressed, the usual blouse, a light tan from rebark dye, the front tied tight with a leather string. She matched it with a skirt of the same hue, and a pair of her leather brogues. Using the polished surface of a thin metal circlet she had purchased with some of her prizes from previous hunts, she made sure to check her auburn hair was not too unruly. Quickly running a brush through it a few times, she gave up on it, pulling the short hair back and holding it in place with a carved wooden clip shaped in the image of an oak leaf that had been a gift from Keemre. Happy enough, with her appearance, she half ran to the big house, worried at how long she had kept the wise woman waiting already.

To her surprise, as she stepped out of the blinding light from the noonday sun and into the shaded front room of the large wooden building, the shadows that she assumed to be Keemre and her apprentices evolved into Keemre and two stranger's she did not know. They both wore the many gold bangles that announced their rank as wise women, each one representing time spent serving a clann. Like Keemre, they also had several further pieces of jewellery decorating their person, the left one sporting a boar head carved with care from what appeared to be some form of shellfish, the other sporting many golden flowers twined around her forehead. Whoever they were, they were important people.

"Alix, please sit down. This is Erikisa from clann Maigh and my mentor, Sruna from clann Laire. They wished to speak with you". Alix moved gingerly and sat on the cushion placed for her in front of them all. She heard rustling behind her and turning, she saw that someone, likely one of Keemre's apprentices, had moved to shut the door, allowing the wooden slates to close off the house and the last of the light. A low *shunk* followed as it was locked. Erikisa leaned forward and, pulling a coal from a sandbox, used it to light a tallow candle placed between them on a low table, normally reserved for Keemre's random assortment of trinkets and papers.

"Alix, I have asked my sisters to be here so we can... counsel you". It appeared Keemre had not simply gone to trade. Alix looked from one wise woman to another noticing the same motherly expression on them all, but a tinge of fear seemed to be evident on the youngest, Erikisa's face.

"Counsel me how"? She asked. Keemre opened her mouth to respond, but Sruna cut her off.

"You have seen magik child". Sruna, for all her appearance as a motherly figure, had a voice like hard aged oak. Her hair, a colour closer to white than grey, was at odds with the darker browns and black of both Erikisa and Keemre. Her eyes were brown and deep to Erikisa's grey and Keemre's green, the twin of Alix's.

"Magik is a dangerous child and when a child takes interest in magik or if magik takes an interest in a child, we grow concerned".

"Tell us, child, your story of the hunt, and what happened. Leave nothing out, you do not know what may be important but we do" Erikisa delivered her request with a smile, likely meant to put Alix at ease, but Alix could see the fear in her eyes, barely hidden.

So Alix retold the hunt, the Great Wolf that had appeared, the roar that had thrown her and her cousins off their feet, all the way through to the burning horn. Yet, as she began to explain the feeling the horn had given her, the subtle calling to it, she pulled back. Hiding the truth.

It surprised her, so unused to holding anything back from any wise women, let alone Keemre. The wise women, seeming to be satisfied with her retelling, had only a few follow up questions for her, luckily Keemre's normally constant questions had trained Alix well on how to tell a tale.

"The boys reported the same?" Sruna asked Keemre, who nodded in agreement.

"Then it is likely not the girl creating this mess but something from within the forest itself". Sruna declared. Before Alix had time to feel relieved though Erikisa added her thoughts. "Do not jump to conclusions sister, the girl was present when the boys heard what they did, it very well might be her".

"Sisters, maybe we thank Alix for her helpfulness and allow her back to her day". Keemre said, interrupting Sruna before she could respond to Erikisa's retort.

"Yes, let's. Thank you Alix, you are dismissed" Sruna's voice begged no discussion at the dismissal.

"Thank you dear", Erikisa added. Smiling softly at Alix as she stood to go, one of the apprentices unlocked and opened the thick wood door, allowing her to finally step out back into the light. She paused as the makeshift door settled into place again and for a moment, she thought to push back in, to demand they explain what was going on. But, just as she felt the courage rise, she felt the eyes of the waiting apprentices on her. Their intention clear as day. If we can't sit in, there is no way we are going to let you too.

And so Alix returned to her chores.

***

As the sun began to set in the sky, throwing an orange glaze over the world Alix sat sitting crossed legged under the awning that hung from the wall of her small hut to the prickly trunk of the small Acasha tree, providing much needed shade the tree alone could not provide with its long and sparse leaves. She methodically ran a series of three hard stones soaked in water over her grandfather's father's blade. There were slight differences in the rocks in the way they felt against her skin. Keemre had shown her this skill of sharpening, using the rougher stone first over the edge of the blade, fifty strokes, before moving to the coarse stone, fifty more, then finally finishing with the smooth stone.

Keemre had no metal tools, and she had learned sharpening during her apprenticeship. And as no other clann member could dream of trading for a metal tool, Alix was grateful for the assistance. In the early days, back when Alix still remembered her life before, she had found the large spearhead hidden at the back of the hovel she had shared with Keemre. It had been wrapped in tough reeds and placed under the thick woven carpet that made the base of Keemre's bed. It had not looked like it did now. Back then, it had been all brown with rust and too dull to be of use.

Keemre had shown her how to care for it, how to bind it to a staff, how to throw it, how to fight with it. Alix had grown to have an uneasy respect for the spear. It was her birthright, apparently, the only thing her parent's had been able to pass on to her and she cherished and cared for it as if doing so in some way showed she cherished their memories.

That is, If I could remember them she thought, feeling that all too familiar feeling begin to rise in her chest. That sense of dread and pain and, above all, loneliness. She put down the wet stone and sat back against the wall of her home, stretching her legs now stiff out in front of her. She didn't want to think about her family or how lonely she was in this world right now, the nagging dispear all to similar to the feeling the Great Wolf had dragged up in her.

A flash of reflected light caught her attention and looking out down the hard packed dirt path she saw the three wise women heading to the edge of the village, their many beaded and jewelled hands scattering light as it caught the light of the ever descending sun. Could the two wise women from the other clanns be leaving so soon? And so late? Surely with all their talk of danger they should wait until the sunrise. Alix rose and, in a mix of curiosity and a desire to not be alone with her thoughts, headed down the hill after the women.

Chapter 3

Alix jogged towards the two visiting women, who were now loudly arguing, a gaggle of apprentices stood a few steps back, looking everywhere but at the two blistering women. Their long, matching flax robes blowing in the wind caught the dying light, causing odd shaped shadows to play across the grass of the village green, making it seem as if the two wise women had stopped for a heated conversation beside a violently thrashing cloud. Alix thought she saw a flash of red within the roiling fabrics, but whatever had caught her eye was quickly obscured as the robes bunched as one, catching a particularly strong gust of wind.

Alix momentarily looked down, dodging the old knotted root that had tripped many a clann member, and as she caught sight of the women again, she stopped suddenly in her tracks. Several of the apprentices appeared to be crouched around something on the ground. From this distance, Alix could not make out what had caught their interest, but whatever it was had drawn the wise women from their private conversation, and the two were quickly bustling to the noticeably more frantic group of apprentices.

"What's going on?" came a voice at her shoulder, despite herself, Alix jumped at the interruption. Jason stood beside her, shading his eyes as he squinted at the now much louder group of women.

"I don't know". Alix mumbled, momentarily embarrassed at being caught off guard.

"Want to check it out?" Her cousin grinned his acknowledgement, and the two continued down the hill, though at a much slower pace.

The women were beginning to head back up the hill carrying whatever it was that had captured their interest, and as they approached, Alix's curiosity was quickly satiated, and a familiar tension of fear sprung to the forefront. They were carrying an apprentice, Maxar, one of Keemre's. The woman's white robe was stained a deep burgundy, and a long yard-long shaft stood out straight from her chest.

"Run! Away!" Keemre was screaming flinging her hands wide as they approached. At who Alix was unsure of, she felt rooted to her spot.

"What happened?" she managed in a voice that sounded much shriller than she thought it should. As if to answer her question, a shaft bloomed through the chest of a second apprentice, showering Alix in blood and getting in her eyes and mouth. Suddenly, screaming was all around her, blinded by the blood that seemed to burn her eyes, she felt more than saw the rush of bodies as people frantically began to scatter. She felt someone grab her hand, Jason attempting to pull her in one way, but Alix's hand, slick with the blood from the slain apprentice, slipped from their grasp, and Alix was pushed to the ground, the air knocked from her.

She gasped and rolled on the ground, rubbing at her eyes, trying to clear them as panic, first fearful, now desperate, seemed just about to overtake her. Receiving a kick from an unseen fleeing person, Alix coughed and wept, still unable to catch her breath, and reaching behind her, she began to crawl off the path. She pulled herself into the drainage ditch, overgrown in sharp grasses that pierced and cut her skin as she pulled herself deeper until her bleeding, bruised hands met the cool water that was gently flowing over the smooth rocks that made up the ground of the riverbed.

Alix splashed her face repeatedly, frantically wiping the already congealing blood from her eyes as the screams around her continued to rise. Eyes finally free from blood, she turned her bruised face to take her first look at what was happening to her village.

Along the palisades that surrounded the village, long limbed creatures stood, their abnormally long legs grasping the wooden stakes, holding them upright as they continued launching yard long arrows into the village from bows that appeared as tall as they were. From the distance, she could not see their faces, but Alix could easily tell that each one stood at a minimum, twice as tall as she.

One of the monsters, pointed a long thin finger into the village, a second sending an arrow in the indicated direction. Alix let out an involuntary sob as she saw the arrows take someone from behind sinking almost halfway through them. The person collapsed and Alix covered her mouth to hide the sobbing as crawled deeper into the weeds, hating herself for trying to hide as she crawled up the overgrown ditch as screaming continued all around her. A splash behind her made her turn screaming, but it was not the face of the giant beast that stared back at her, but her cousin, his eyes already glazed over, a long blue arrowhead standing clear from his neck. The tip dripped droplets of blood into the quickly polluted stream.

This was all too much, Alix opened her mouth to scream again, but nothing came. She collapsed into the muddy side of the ditch, all her energy draining from her as violence and terror continued all around her. Her silent sobs overtook her and she lay there, even overcome as she was, she still hid her mouth behind her hands, her knuckles white, fists shaking as she lost herself to her fear.

She stayed where she lay, her clothes now saturated with the mud and filth carried by the stream. The weeds and grasses that grew out of the muddy soil mostly hid her from view and with knees drawn to her chest Alix shuddered as the violence continued all around her.

I am a coward. She told herself, and it hurt all the more because it was true. All around her, her clann, her family and friends screamed in fear in pain, and she lay, crying, like a wounded child.

Time passed and suddenly, she realised the only sound she could hear was her own. The realisation caught the next sob in her throat and she half gagged as she attempted to force herself to breathe. Her body still shaking, she cautiously raised her head and looked behind her, to the still motionless body of her cousin. Her face was now covered by shadows, saving Alix the pain of having to see his lifeless eyes staring back at her. Slowly, careful not to brush against the vegetation in case she drew attention to her hiding place, she began to crawl once again back up the ditch, laying low in the muddy water. Once she would have been devastated to have stained her favourite flax tunic. That thought seemed immaterial now.

Coming to a turn in the ditch, Alix braved a look. Her first attempt was too quick, and with her heart pumping fast and loud enough that her body seemed to be vibrating, she did not risk a second glance until she got a handle on her breathing. Sitting back into the ditch she tried again the breathing exercise Keemre had taught her as a child, back in those early days when the memories of her parent's loss still haunted her dreams.

Keemre had been so kind, holding her as her little body shook with sobs, her throat raw as sandpaper as she clung to Keemre's faded tunic as if she was being pulled from shore by a great storm and the spindly kind woman was the only branch to grab, a worn but strong anchor in the night. '*There there child'*, she would murmur as she stroked her hair. *'I am right here, I am right here'*. She would repeat.

Except she wouldn't any longer. Would never again. *No Stop that!* She scolded herself, Keemre would not want her to sit here and cry over her, not yet. Safety first, Cry second. She reminded herself, one of Keemre's favourite sayings to the children as they ran through the brush and grasslands that had until recently made up her universe. The universe now seemed a lot bigger.

She took one final deep breath in, letting it out slowly and surprising herself at the steadyness of it. She no longer sounded like a terrified little girl, more like a terrified long-range runner, breath still shaky, but much more consistent, and measured. She risked now, a second glance over the lip of the ditch, rising slowly enough that she hoped the movement was not noticed by any waiting monsters.

The large monsters still stood around the village square, several of them still resting on the top of the palisades, long legs bent to hunker down low to the wall, mighty curved bows still in hand. Now having some time to study the monsters she realized something shocking about their green fur that seemed to cover their bodies, it was moss. Moss of such strains and colours that each monster seemed to be a multitude of greens and blues, browns and yellows. The moss appeared to cover all of their bodies from their large arms to equally large legs, the only part of their oddly shaped frames that did not seem to be covered by this thick carpet of moss where their heads which instead bore large dark wooden masks that obscured what Alix assumed could only be hideously grotesque faces. They were all lacquered, seeming to glow from the firelight of the torches, each one was carved with intricate markings that Alix could not make out from this distance.

What Alix could see though, what was unavoidable to her, was the tall man standing in the middle, the one who had killed Keemre. He seemed small standing as he was surrounded by those monsters, but comparing him to the mass of huddled people being herded into the village centre, his height could not be more than just above average.

He wore only a simple tunic, tied at his waist, brandishing a short spear with which he was gestating wildly to the beasts as they followed his bidding. He had hair curly like her own but cut in a peculiar pattern. Worn short, it was shaved to the scalp on the side and back, the tight curls worn up on his head, tied in some sort of knot to keep it out of his eyes. His ears pointed in a way that Alix felt was unnatural. His skin was not as fallow as her own, sickly white-like skin not used to seeing the sun. And all over he was tattooed, wild terrifying shapes inked into his skin that even at this distance made the figure seem like some form of demon, set upon her home to kill and destroy.

The village square seemed to be filling up now as the beasts began to bring the last of the survivors into the opening. Alix watched as the tattooed man pointed his spear directing the moss monsters who pushed the terrified villages along, as they allowed themselves to be herded into separate groups, watched over by the monsters.

Tearing her eyes away from the terrified faces of her neighbours, her people, she sought out her hut. From her hiding hole in the ditch, she could see that there was a route through now. If she could get there, get her bow and… that part of the plan hadn't come to her yet, but she had to do something. She took the first step towards the hut as the image of her, bow in hand, arrow nocked, came to mind. A vision of her dispatching the tattooed man and his monsters and saving her people, but the second step faltered as she once again scanned the area and reassessed her chances. Five, seven, ten beasts and the odd tattooed man made it eleven.

Even if she was able to kill them, and she was most unsure of that, she did not have enough arrows to do so. She froze again, cursing herself as she frantically looked from the village square to her hut and back. Torn between movement and nonmovement, it took a shout from the village centre to spur her to action. The group was now moving out, making their way through a newly torn hole in the palisades towards the forest behind and the distant mountains. It was now or never. Stay safe, stay hidden or attempt to save the only people she cared about. *Fuck it.* She thought and began to move, as quietly as she could, towards home.

Any sense of stealth was long abandoned by the time she fell through the fabric draped over the door frame and fell gasping to the floor. With panic and fear now fully taking hold of her she quickly ran her eyes over the room. There in one corner was her bow, six arrows resting beside it, a further four unfinished on the stool, waiting for an arrowhead of fletching that was unlikely to be coming now. She quickly grabbed up the bow and six usable arrows and turned to leave when a blue glint of light caught her eye. The horn. It seemed to glimmer again as her eyes found it. Magik was afoot once again. *Was it related to the attack?* She thought for only a moment before grabbing that up too, throwing it and the arrows into her leather quiver. It was sharp, she told herself, better to have than not. Cautiously, she moved to the opening of the hut, peering through the gap in the curtain for movement. The village was now quiet.

She jogged in a crouch from the hut, moving down the hill towards the village square, one arrow nocked and ready to loose. Peering past the corner of one building, located right at the corner of the square she relaxed as she saw that no, there was not a band of monsters waiting to ambush her. The relief vanished quickly however as she began to become aware of the bodies that littered the green. Their red blood soaked the ground, leaving puddles of thick red mud around the bodies of her friends and neighbours.

The body of Keemre lay there, her knees neatly pulled towards her chest, eyes closed as if she was sleeping. Alix walked towards her but as she neared, she saw the deep angry gash across her chest, her tunic now stained black with blood. Alix turned away to vomit. She fell to her knees and heaved until only bile came out, and around deep angry sobs she shakily wiped her mouth, careful not to turn and look at Keemre again. *'Safety first, Cry second'.* She said to herself, as she wiped the tears and spit from her face.

"Safety First", she repeated pushing herself to her feet, still shaky but more determined than before.

"Cry second", she said as she turned and walked through the wall that had once protected her people. There were so many dead behind her, but out there there were more still alive. They needed saving. Maybe Alix wouldn't be able to. Maybe she would fail. But she needed to try.

***

31

Following the trail turned out to be quite easy though the beasts appeared to be able to cross vast differences quite easily, the mass of humans they were taking with them could only travel so quickly. Alix camped the first night in a burrow she had found careful to ensure it was already empty before settling in for the short hours she would rest. Dreams took her back to the village the death, the screams the smell of blood and death and the feeling of panic and dread woke her violently. She decided that the first night she would not sleep more than four hours. Just enough to keep her from collapsing from exhaustion, but minimizing the amount of time she had to spend with her mind, and her memories.

The second day showed she was quickly catching up to the party as she came across what appeared to be a campsite. There were the remains of several fires and unfortunately, the bodies of two villagers. Da and Brae Malley, an old couple who had always been kind to her, lay cuddled together in the grass. The woman, Brae, had a bad cut that seemed to have been bandaged, but anyone who would have seen an injury of that like would know it would not be healable.

The old man had no visible wound and his death momentarily perplexed Alix until she noticed some torn leaves poking from a small bag he had at his belt. Foxthorn leaves. A small bit could be used to make tea to help with pain. A large dose was lethal.

Alix took the small leather bag of Foxthorn and tried her best to otherwise leave the couple where they lay, determined to mourn the couple when the rest were free. If she could free them, if not... Well, no need to worry about mourning then. As the days pressed on Alix's determination changed to something new. A sense of momentum kept her moving forward but the hope and determination she had felt now turned, twisted into something darker, more sinister. She was now closing in quickly on the group, they were only a few miles from the forest border and Alix had decided she would make her move before then.

The thick forest of the trees would greatly disadvantage her bow and she was well used to hunting in the long grass, stepping up to loose before ducking behind the flowing vegetation. That meant she needed to make her move today or tomorrow. The fearful part of her, the part that wanted to take the easier option screamed wait one more day, you will be more rested, more ready, but the part of her that was more present, that knew the improbable nature of her undertaking said no. Enough was enough, she would make her stand here.

Maybe she could kill some of them, maybe she could cause a distraction big enough that some would escape. She didn't know what would happen but, she did know she would die. It was odd to her that she was okay with that fact but decided to not dwell on it further as she readied herself for the fight to come.

Alix spotted the lights of the party's campfires as she crested the final hill. The sun would rise soon, within an hour if she had timed this right, and she would strike while it rose behind her, hopefully obscuring herself to do the beasts and the tattooed man who she could now see, from her vantage point, sitting crossed legged at one of the several fires, eating alone. The beasts wandered around the campsite moving supplies and herding captives as they arose. She could see now that many of them were tied together, large hemp ropes binding from one next to the next in long chains of people.

The humans themselves were split into two groups, the main group of humans all seemed to be wearing the same simple long tunic. She could not place its material from this distance but it seemed decidedly plain. They also appeared to have something around their necks, often roped together in groups of four or five, that were now busying themselves among the camp, moving in between the terrifying monsters as if they were not there. The smaller group was made up of people she recognized, faces of her neighbours and friends, some holding terrified children to their chests. They were huddled in a pen as the moss beasts moved among them passing out what Alix could only assume was some form of gruel the beasts were busy heating over cook fires. Unlike the smaller group stayed in their pen. Not one of them made an attempt to rise or move from their spot in the trampled grass. Alix, watched the camp for a while, planning her attack and gauging how long she had before she must act.

The tattooed man rose then and began to lazily stroll through the camp. The beasts, as if aware of his presence, moved out of his way as he strode, no sooner had he turned to face a direction was the path cleared, the monsters ensuring their master was unmolested as he moved towards the pen. With curiosity, she watched as the tattooed figure moved to the sitting humans. He examined them one by one and as he moved on a beast moved forward, painting the human with some sort of coloured paste. There seemed to be no reason for the colour of the paste, at least that Alix could see and she began to wonder about the significance when the tattooed man stopped before a young girl. He reached down and pulled her to her feet. The child did not fight him as she allowed him to pull her up and away from the pen, she could see then the change in the rest of the captives. The bowed heads, and the subservient demeanour were still there, but she could feel the tension build, feel the eyes follow the tattooed man as he led the young girl away from the camp.

Dread and fear once again rose within her breast, she risked a look over her shoulder, seeing now the sun was finally beginning to set behind the hill. It had to be now. She pulled the six arrows from her quiver holding them in her left hand as she picked up her bow, freshly strung with a new waxed string. The horn, now secured tightly to her thigh, bound with an old bowstring that had lost most of its wax coating, she crouched and began her hunt.

Alix kept her head down as she moved across the grass until she was less than a hundred yards from the first campfire, the one the tattooed man had been sitting at alone before he took that young girl. She said a brief thank you to Mother Earth that the grasses were so dense this close to the Darkwood, that she had a myriad of small mounds to hide behind. She took a quick peek to get her bearings now she had safely made it to the camp's edge, and began to circle left, towards the largest of the fires, the one near the pen. Three of the moss monsters were guarding the pen. One lazily sat staring, Alix assumed it had eyes under the haunting oak mask, at the captives, their eyes downcast at the trampled grass. Two more stood at the far end of the enclosure, blocking off the route to the tattooed man.

She didn't dare to look and see where the other seven were, she didn't have enough arrows for them all anyway. *I need to save who I can.* She told herself. These captives were not roped together, they had a better chance of escaping. Being much closed now she could see their hands were bound with the same rope that chained the other captives together, but given enough time most people would be able to escape that rope. She just needed to buy them time. Glancing again back at the route the man had stolen the girl down Alix readied herself, before turning back to the easier and only available option before her. The three monsters that watched the captives had yet to move, so quickly she decided her order of shots, took a deep breath in, loosening her shoulders, and as she breathed out, she stood.

The first arrow took the first of the monster in the back of its moss-covered head, at only a few yards away, the arrow buried itself deep, making a wet crunch like rotted wood as it sank deep. The monster did not so much as move from its sitting position and Alix had a second to worry she couldn't stop these horrors before its head tilted forward and the stillness of death became evident. She then took sight of the other two, both of which had not yet noticed the fate of their ally. She placed the second arrow just below the mask of one of the creatures, it crumbling to the ground, large hands going to what on a human Alix would have called its throat.

Alix hooked a third arrow and took the final beast in its breast. It faltered and fell to its knees, mask quickly swinging to and fro searching for the hidden shots Alix finished it with a fourth arrow sinking into the exposed back of its head as its mask turned frantically silent and searching for its assailant, for her. She rushed to the pen now, knocking over the frankly, weakly stacked wooden fence and barrelled into the centre of the pen.

All eyes were on her now. Shocked expressions stared at her as if she was the monster out of a late-night story and not those who lay dead around them. "Run!" she said in a half screech, half whisper. That shocked the watching faces into action and as one boy stood and ran for the opening, suddenly they all were. A horrible wail went up towards the centre of camp, away from Alix's hastily made exit and she turned in time to see several, perhaps the remaining living beasts, all sprinting towards her. Two of the herd peeled off and ran towards the hole in the fence arms wide as if in an attempt to capture the fleeing captives.

Alix spent her last two arrows taking both down, one through its leg, for which it toppled like a felled tree, the other through its neck, dropping it instantly. As soon as the last arrow was loosed she turned and ran not after the fleeing villagers, her people, but instead to the collapsed bodies of the two creatures furthest from the army of horrors that were now almost atop her. She managed to make it to the first grabbing and ripping the arrow that had stood proud from its chest before an enormous hand hit her, lifting her off the ground and sending her flailing through the air to land on the opposite side of the pen's fence. She had a moment of shocked confusion before she began to crawl frantically to the grass's edge, then throwing herself into a run. The horrifying brawing of the monsters at her back.

But she was not running in the same direction she had come, the direction the captives now fled. Instead, as she managed to get to her feet, she ran head first into the tattooed man. He was covered from head to toe in red paint and before him, a small hollow held a dark pool of the same hue and shade. With sudden horror she screamed at the realization. Not paint, blood. Knowing then in a way her mind tried to reject, that the small pool, the blood which now coated the tattooed man, was that of the little girl.

He smiled at her then, recognizing in her face the conclusion she had just made, basking in the hate and disgust that she had for him. He spread his arms wide and laughed. A deep cruel sound that seemed to tear at her skin. Without thinking she loosed her last arrow at his chest, knowing as she did it the monsters behind would tear her apart. Hoping that those who escaped could stay free, and take it back home, knowing that the rest of the captives likely would not escape now.

The arrow exploded as it hit his exposed flesh. The flint tip shattered into innumerable pieces as the haft, continuing along its course splintered against the blood-drenched man. He laughed again and Alix stumbled back falling onto her back as the tattooed man moved towards her.

"You would make great *Saer"* he crooned as he watched her, noticing and savouring the fear in her eyes. His accent was songlike, a harsh tone that seemed to boom against her ears. Several of the monsters now surrounded her, he glanced at them and then wordlessly turned back to camp.

"You speak my tongue?" she said with shock, he spat a laugh back in response. "You speak my language you dirty rat, you simply have forgotten who your masters are". Each word was delivered with menace. "You may have freed some *Saer*, but no matter they will be caught again, the taste of *Saer* is just too... intoxicating". Alix stared up at this man, who smiled so wickedly at her, who wore the blood of a child on his body as if he had bathed in it, and imagined him bathing in her blood, the blood of her friends.

"No", she managed.

The tattooed man smiled again. "What was that?" he said leaning forward towards the beaten girl. "I couldn't hear you?" he said, his voice like thick honey. His words seemed to reverberate across her skin. The tattooed man now leered over her, the now drying blood peeling and falling onto her as he moved. Up close she could see his markings better, see what it was this man had devoted his skin to displaying. All over his chest were images of pain, of people being torn apart, ripped in two. Of people dead and dying, of them being killed, being tortured. And, throughout the intricate tellings of violence, others were rejoicing, long-eared figures feasting on the dead, on the dying, committing horrible acts of violence and pain. It was her future, the future of her entire clann, this man would do all these things to her, to them.

"No," she said again, louder than before. The man laughed again and slapped her down to the earth, laying a soft hide boot on her chest.

"No?" He laughed, "Saer cannot say no, they only obey". He purred, stroking a tattooed finger under her chin. Pushed to the ground, Alix shifted uncomfortably, but the tattooed man, not a man, a monster, did not budge. "I do love a fighter," he said, "maybe I shall have you fight some of your little friends". He continued to caress her face, moving to her hair as he spoke. "So pretty". He growled, low, hungrily.

Something was sticking into her leg, something sharp and Alix remembered the horn. This monster was annihilation made flesh, she must protect her clann, she must! Grabbing the horn, now shockingly hot to the touch, she looked into the tattooed man's eyes once more. She saw only a bottomless depth of darkness staring back at her.

"You will not have them!" she screamed and with a violent tug of her arm, the horn was free and with all the strength left to her, all the hope of survival gone and feeling nothing but grim acceptance, she raised the horn and buried it down through the collar bone of the man. The horn sank deep, the tip burrowing into the chest of the evil man as the fluted end stood majestically out of the space between his head and his shoulder.

Alix was surprised the horn had pierced his skin at all but that shock was quickly replaced as out of the horn came what Alix could only describe as a flood of dark black blood. The tattooed man shrieked then, rising to his feet only long enough to fall once again as his lifeblood flowed quickly out of the horn, like a cask of mead being tapped. He swayed on all fours, as Alix kicked herself back from him, he managed to raise his head one final time, and Alix saw the shock there, the pain, the fear. And she spat in his face as he died.

She let her head fall back into the tough grass as she tried to catch her breath, she heard the moss monsters before she saw them and they slowly surrounded the spot where she and her prey lay. They would probably kill her now. She chuckled at that as her eyes closed and exhaustion took her.

Chapter 4

Alix awoke in the Pen; her hands were bound, and as she awoke, still in the throes of her daily nightmare, she began to flail wildly, her lungs trying to scream past the rope knot that filled her mouth. "It's okay! It is okay!" came a raspy voice behind her, and for a moment, she thought it was Keemre before looking back into the hard, stone eyes of Sruna.

Despite herself, Alix flinched and tried to rise but found she couldn't. Sruna spoke before Alix could dwell further on that fact.

"Try not to move, young one, your body is bruised, and you are tied down. After you killed that… that man, you passed out. The *Sluagh* didn't seem to know what to do with you, we thought they had killed you at first, laid you here as a warning to us. But, they tied you down and well… Well, you live, child, and that is something to be grateful for. I think what you did was incredibly heroic, girl, but mule-headed stupid". Alix tried to look up at the wizened woman, but her head swam, and she instead rested it back upon the now well-trampled grass. Instead, she asked a question. "*Sluagh*?"

"Trapped spirits of the dead, child. Pay attention. They have been standing over there around the corpse of their master for hours now". Sruna said, her voice like rough sand over stone. Alix noticed now how different her face looked from only a few days prior; hollow, pale, her hard eyes no longer had that strict authority of a disciplinary. No, instead, it was the hardness of the damned. Alix had seen those eyes once before. Several years ago when, a nearby clann had sentenced a man to die. Her clann had gone to the ceremony, the man had the same look as he was brought forward, had had the same look up until the end.

Sruna looked concerned and was now bent over her, eyes searching her own. She became aware of Sruna's voice but could not seem to piece the sounds into words. The last thing she thought before slipping into unconsciousness was how odd it was that someone who she had for such a brief time could look at her with such worry.

Alix awoke next to the vast blanket of stars staring down at her. For a moment, she felt like she was falling towards those bright lights in the night, rushing up towards the heavens. She blinked several times, feeling much stronger than she had before and took stock of her situation. Her hands were bound, as were her legs, but her head was free. She looked around herself and saw the sleeping bodies around the pen. Her vision was limited, unable to see past the nearest huddled bodies, but it looked like at least some people had escaped. A tightness in her chest she didn't know was there finally relaxed, and she let out a sigh of relief. Whatever her fate, her sacrifice was not for nought.

She looked over the nearby bodies, trying to see if she could recognise them by their silhouettes in the starlight. She spied what Sruna had referred to; the beast stood in a group over the corpse of the dead man, the man she had killed. She waited to see how that felt and was surprised by how much it didn't. The man was a monster, a fiend that had attacked and killed her people, who had stolen away so many from their homes and had done... the man had done something awful to that little girl. It was right to kill him, wasn't it? To want to end him. Yet she didn't feel accomplished. She didn't really feel anything. She decided to put that aside for later. It was not the time to dwell on what that might mean for her.

Sruna stroked her hair, and it brought Alix back to earth. "How long?" she said, or rather, attempted to say. The moss creatures - the *Sluagh* - had done a number to her. She didn't know how bad her face appeared, but from Sruna's flinching reaction and the way the other captives avoided looking at her, she knew it must not be good. "You were unconscious for a while, child, I do not know for how long, but night is not far away now". She was right, of course, as Alix lay there on the damp grass, she could see the shadows were now long black ink across the grassland, it would not be long before the sun went away and her sister moon rose.

·   "What do they want with us?" Alix mumbled through swollen and ripped lips. Sruna did not respond, looking away towards the sinking sun for a moment that stretched long enough that Alix began to wonder if Sruna had not heard her. She opened her mouth to talk again, causing herself to wince, and that brought Sruna back to her as she shushed Alix and gently stroked her face.

"Keemre hadn't told you of the *Sluagh* then? Not surprising, apprentices only learn of *Na Fírinne* later in their instruction". Alix went to shake her head. She was not Keemre's apprentice, and she never would be now, but Sruna was not looking at her and so continued. "*Na Fírinne* is the truth of the world child, the truth of all that is and will be. It is… extensive, child. Not a history nor a prophecy but… it is the truth of it". Sruna was silent for a moment before continuing,

"The important bits for you to know is what has happened and what will happen next. That man you killed, he is not a man, Alix, he is one of the *Aos Si*, the old ones, the first peoples, Fae!" her voice rose as she spoke, the terror so far kept at bay breaking through, "they hunt us, like animals, to them that is all we are, prey. The *Sluagh* are their spawn, creatures created by death to bring death. They come when the veils between our worlds are at their weakest, when their magik allows them to enter our world, and they come, they hunt, and they take those they capture away… We do not know what happens to those they take. But they never return". Sruna's hand was still stroking her face but harder and faster than before, the woman taken by the demons of her imagination.

"I think the Fae was taking us home, to his home, but you stopped him, now we are trapped here." Alix noticed the shoulders of those huddled nearby drop lower. "Escape," Alix managed, "I killed some of them". Sruna shook her head sadly, "Look again, child," she whispered. Alix once again spied the group of beasts, of the *Sluagh*, and started as she noticed the dark wood arrows sticking out from several of them, the ones she had felled. One was casually pulling one of her arrows from its torso while another helped its comrade pull an arrow free from the back of its head. Alix felt her heartbeat rise as the weight of that fact settled on her. "Oh," she said, "I think I am…" She did not finish her sentence as her body pushed beyond its limits allowed her mind to once again swim into unconsciousness.

As she awoke for the third time, was it the third? Things were immediately different. Loud, angry voices shouted in gruff voices, Sruna, who had sat by her side the entire time, was now cowed against the fence with the rest of the captives, only she remained in the centre of the pen. Looking around desperately, she located once again the group of *Sluagh*. They stood where they had before, still unmoving, though the beasts she had pierced seemed to have by now removed the offending arrows. But what caused her blood to chill was the sight of the two new guests among them. Two men with long hair, shaved at the sides and tied in a bun upon their heads, exposing long pointed   ears.

They wore stylised tattoos across their arms, their chest covered by a leather vest of a peculiar blend of beige and tan. At their waists hung ugly, hand-sized blades, the shorter of which kept stroking longingly as he listened to the other bellow in his face. She moved almost involuntarily, as if her body had decided to need to run before she had the time to make the decision, but tied down as she was, all she managed was to pound her feet against the earth. That brought silence to the two men who now were both staring at her, their eyes seeming to glow in the dark light of the moon. Alix began to kick wildly and began to scream,

"Sruna! Sruna, Help!" but the woman did not look up, her eyes fixed on the ground in front of her. As one, the two Fae slinked towards her, like foxes to a bird with a broken wing.

As they approached, the shorter one stopped a foot behind the taller as he leaned down to peer into her eyes. "This is the insect that killed Kadir? It cannot be old enough to see several moons!" his accent was not as deep as the dead one's, but it retained the singsong quality. He stood and leaned back, letting out a harsh, loud bark of a laugh.

"Oh, this is rich, I can already tell the stories at court will be tasty, powerful ones, don't you agree, Beag?" the smaller one grunted his response, a neutral and much deeper tone.

"Yes, this tithing will be rich with stories for us". He said with as much enthusiasm as a wet rock. He leaned down to Alix until his nose was almost ready to touch hers. Alix did not move a muscle, terrified that anything she did could be her last. "The court will be very eager to meet you," He crooned.

"I suspect Kadir put up a fight, of course, given your appearance, but I promise you, those pains will pair in comparison to what you will experience with me". He smiled wide, hungrily and nipped at her, causing her to flinch, much to his delight.

"Can't." said the smaller man, Beag, "By Bronan's law, she is not yours to keep, she was Kadir's trophy, not yours, Mort". The larger man spun on the other, roaring with terrible fury at the smaller man.

"Who are you to tell me what is mine and what is not? Kadir is dead, I now lead the hunt". Beag continued to stroke the blade at his belt. "You do," he agreed. But Bronan's law is clear: the captives are Kadir's, they transfer to the court first, not you". Mort roared again at Beag, but the smaller fae did not flinch. "Very well, Beag, he who thinks so highly of the laws of Bronan. Let us away to court, and you may explain to Fiachra why his brother is dead. He does so enjoy your company". Mort finished with a sneer, and Beag snarled quietly, revealing a set of two twin sharp canines. Mort laughed again, leaning back to bark it upward before spinning to the still waiting *Sluagh*. "Take them!" he shouted gesturing to Alix and the other captives, "We away!".

Chapter 5

The journey was brutal, the Fae led from the front, running and darting too and forth, the *Sluagh* leading the captives behind, Alix now added to the rope chain that connected groups of captives. The Fae seemed to disappear at times, running far ahead and returning to shout commands at the *Sluagh*, always with the final command of *Hurry!* The *Sluagh* took all the harassment in silence. She had heard them roar, but it appeared they did not have speech. It was not obvious where they were being taken, the large trees of the deep woods slowly coming into view as the harried group continued their trek across the plain.

It wasn't long until they were within them, constantly pulled by their necks by the *Sluagh*, the captives flinching at the laughs and commands from the Fae. Alix could barely keep up, falling several times, though she was proud of herself as, despite her current condition, she was not the one who fell the most often, and she was always first back on her feet, quick to avoid the cold hard grasp of the *Sluagh* as they yanked the captives back to their feet, each time wondering if the almost indistinguishable *Sluagh* was one she had shot if it felt any anger towards her for doing so. The same unblinking wooden masks of the creatures seemed to say no, but she did not know the rules of magik beasts and decided it mattered not if they did or didn't they were all being led to fate, this court that Mort and Beag spoke of, a place she thought, maybe the home of *Aos Si,* maybe the home of Kadir the Fae she had slain.

Within a day, they were deep in the forest and began to climb, the ground starting to slope, first gradually, then quite dramatically, forcing the captives and their silent escorts to slow considerably as they strove forward. Beag and Mort stayed with the group now, sitting alone when the group rested, staying at the head of the column as they moved. They seemed tense, Mort still shouting at Beag, but there was less heat in that before. A definite nervous energy had settled on them and, from there, had seeped into the captives. By the time the temperature had dropped enough that Alix could feel her teeth chatter, she began to wonder if she would make it to this mythical court or if they would all die from the cold before. Before long, her unasked question was answered as the group slowed and stopped before a large cliff face, reaching off into the clouds.

The two Fae were, as usual, arguing amongst themselves, this time though Beag seemed to be standing his ground, refusing whatever it was Mort was asking of him in increasingly desperate pleas. In the end, it seemed Beag won the argument as, with a roar, Mort stamped towards the cliff face and laid both his hands upon it, lowering his head to rest against it. Alix huddled in the snow that had now begun to pile up around them, watched curiously through bruised eyes as Mort spoke softly under his breath against the wall before lifting his head and striding back to the group. The rock face seemed to crack, and the mountain itself seemed to bend as where Mort had stood, a passageway began to appear, the mountain seeming to stretch itself open. The humans all gazed in wonder at Mort, who was now leaning one hand against the wall of the newly formed tunnel sweating as he tried to catch his breath. *Magik*, she thought to herself, amazed. Once Mort had righted himself, he led the procession through, Beag for the first time following last.

The passage was warmer than the outside, though not wide enough to walk abreast. There was no light for which to see, and so Alix had to stumble along, being guided only by the rope tugging at her neck and her fellow captive pushing behind.

They continued for at least another twenty minutes, the temperature rising noticeably until Alix began to sweat. Then, all of a sudden, they stepped out of the passage and into the blinding light.

Alix's mouth fell open, and she heard the gasps of her fellow captives as they took in the seemingly inconceivable view they were presented with. Before them stretched a valley of such greenery that they had never seen. Snow-packed peaks surrounded the deep valley, a large river of pure blue and white running the length of it. The edges of the valley were dressed with white birch trees, each one larger than Alix had ever seen before, their leaves large and vibrantly green against the snow. Along the river sat squat stone buildings of a burnished white stone that seemed to gleam, each one seeming to have large decorative gardens of colourful fruits and flowers of all shades. Large one-horned goats grazed lazily in the grass, short and green, between homes.

"It's beautiful" Alix breathed. Sruna coughed beside her. "It is not for us child". She whispered. "Remember that". It was the first time Sruna had spoken to her since their forced march, and Alix felt an odd mixture of longing for the woman's company and anger at the way she had ignored her cries for help. Alix opened her mouth to respond, but the *Sluagh* holding her rope pulled her as the procession began their descent down the mountain along the paved path through the valley. As they approached the first of the buildings, the finery of it came into greater focus. Each face of the stone bricks used to create the building was intricately carved with images of rain, flowers, and dancing. Alix had never seen images so expertly created in her life and marvelled at the skill, the time it must have taken to create such works of art.

She wasn't the only one. Though Mort, still leading their party, kept his eyes locked straight ahead, the captives gazed slack-jawed at the opulence on display. A building came up on their right; a large wooden wheel spun lazily. It sat within the fast-flowing river, and up close, Alix could see the slated pieces of wood that caught the water, turning the wheel. She wondered what it was for. Was this some sort of art piece like the carvings or some odd magik like the tunnel through the cave that brought them here. Shortly, it became clear that the odd building was their destination, and as Mort led them up the carved stone steps and past the tall stained walls that enclosed the building and a large square of land within, she saw the others.

Alix didn't notice them at first, instead she walked into the back of the person infront of her, her eyes too busy scanning the carved birds that made up the fluted columns of the square. Horrified gasps pulled her gaze back to ground level and her mind seemed to jump as it took in what she and the other new arrivals saw before them. Dozens of other humans hurried across the square, carrying sacks into one building and back out again. In the courtyard, men and women, each with a collar of metal clasped firmly around their necks, tossed heaps of wheat in the wind, separating the grain from the chaff. Though the building itself was no larger than the big house in her village, the compound itself enclosed an area at least twice the size of the village. Mort led them over to a corner where an angry-looking Fae watched over children, collared the same as the rest, as they beat the cut wheat against the inside of clay pots. A large dagger sat at his waist, and he flexed and stretched a wicked length of cord, a barbed whip, in his hands. A message that the group of new captives instantly recognised and understood. He was far more heavily tattooed than either Mort or Beag but nowhere near as decorated as the one she had killed, Kadir. *Does knowing his name make what she did harder?* She still felt as if she should feel remorse, yet none came. *Good,* she thought.

Mort went to speak to the Fae, this overseer of the human captives, and shortly, several smaller Fae ran from the far barracks. Their hair was not shaved or tied tightly on their heads instead, it hung long and unbound, and that was not the only difference in their appearance. While the Fae she had seen so far wore leathers and went bare-chested, these Fae wore flowing white garments, almost translucent as the sun caught them, displaying bodies bare of any marking.

Each of the Fae was holding several dozen collars of a similar make to the ones around the necks of the enslaved humans, they wordlessly moved among the captives, cutting them free from their bonds before snapping the collar around their neck and pushing them to their knees. Most took this most recent act of bondage in silence, though some, sick of the disgrace that they had been forced to bear these past days, attempted to struggle, though the small fae, some of which appeared to be women, violently and quickly beat down any opposition and within a few minutes the majority of her group sat collared on the ground.

A young fae woman approached Alix then, pausing and frowning once she noticed the condition of her face. She smirked, obviously amused by the pain wrought on her and raised her small dagger to cut her rope bonding when Beag was there grasping her wrist while the knife was still at her neck. "She's for the court". Was all he said, but the knowing smirk that engulfed the Fae woman's face set Alix's blood to run cold.

She turned instead to Sruna and cut the old woman's bondage quickly, placing the collar around Sruna's neck quickly, and Sruna fell to her knees before the Fae was able to push her. Alix tried to catch Sruna's eye, try to ask all the questions in her mind with her gaze, but Sruna's head stayed bowed. In a way, she thought that was the answer enough.

Within moments, Alix stood alone among the group. Her kin and neighbours were kneeling all around her, collared with heads bowed. Beag pulled her back, then, towards the entrance. Despite her better judgement, she struggled, trying to stay with the only group of people she had ever known, but Beag's strength was such that he did not register her protests, simply continuing as Mort finished his conversation with the overseer and moved to join them. The overseer, turning now to his free batch of captives, spoke.

"You are all property of the court. You will stay here, you will work here, and after your short lives have ended, you will be buried here". He began to walk among them, flexing the whip in his hands as the younger Fae watched on. "I am the Feitheoir, the Overseer of this mill, you will obey me or suffer the consequences",... he continued, flanked now by the *Sluagh* creatures who stood stoically, watching over the captives, but the rest of his speech was lost to Alix as Beag pulled her back through the opening in the wall and back down the stone steps and onto the carved path.

Alone with the two Fae, as they continued to pull her further from all she had known, everyone she had loved and cared for, Alix found the courage to speak, though the pain she still felt caused the words to come out as a collection of mumbled syllables. "What?" Beag asked, pausing on the path to turn to her. She swallowed and tried again. "What happens to them?" she asked. Beag opened his mouth to answer, but it was Mort who responded first. "Better than what is about to happen to you, vermin". He sneered before turning and continuing down the path. Beag paused a moment, seeming to wrestle with a desire to answer the question and a general apathy towards her. "They are *thráill,* slaves". He said, shrugging in a way that spoke to the obviousness of that fact.

"They won't be mistreated, but they will be forced to work, that is the nature of us and you, we dominate and rule, you suffer and survive". He turned then and yanked on her rope, forcing her to have to run to catch up lest she end up in a heap on the ground. "And me? What happens to me?" She tried, but Beag did not answer. Up ahead, Mort barked a grim laugh.

They passed by more buildings as they journeyed through the valley, each one as intricately carved as the next and as they climbed, the sun now high in the sky, approaching midday, Alix began to see people move from their homes, many coming to look at their odd procession with odd amusement as they passed. Very few of the Fae they passed had any markings at all, though they all shared the long, curly red-brown hair that fell in waves past their shoulders. Their near-transparent tunics of white gently moved with the subtle breeze that seemed to flow down from the mountains.

Though Alix kept her eyes down, feeling the predatory gazes of those she passed, she was able to spy another distinction between these normal, if normal was indeed the correct word, Fae and her captives. Beyond the tattooing, the harsh leathers and the odd hairstyles, all their eyes were amber, very different to the red of Beag and Mort. And Kadir, she reminded herself. Despite herself, she was curious why that was so, but a part of her knew that this curiosity was more than likely just an attempt by her mind to distract from her impending doom, the destruction of her life, death of friends and family and being thrown headfirst into an entirely alien reality. She had heard stories of brave heroes charging head first into the lion's den to rescue their love, facing certain death without fear. In this moment, however, she was unsure how anyone could possibly accomplish that.

As they passed another collection of buildings, nestled together around a swelling in the river that formed a large lake that seemed to stretch across the length of the valley, the three of them took a turn of the path and began to climb a gentle slope up the mountain. It then became apparent where their final destination would be. Nestled between two peaks in the range, a large stone wall stood, enclosing an area Alix thought must be equal to all the buildings they had passed combined. Standing tall above the wall was a round tower, pushing towards the sky, seeming to pierce the clouds. Mort turned to look at her then. "Welcome to your grave, vermin". He said, and with a sharp bark, he began to scale the gentle slope towards the fortress.

Beag continued to pull her behind, assured that Alix, bound as she was, could do nothing but follow or be dragged upward. As they approached, she could feel her heartbeat quicken. She told herself it was only the activity that what seemed certain death at the top of the path could somehow be survived. She gazed behind her, trying to catch a glimpse of the compound where what was left of her kin were confined to, a Mill, the overseer had called it. But even with the vantage they now had, climbing as they were, she could not make much out through the dense foliage of the birch forest, seeming to spread from the walls of the mountains to cover the majority of the valley.

As they approached, the sun began to dip. It had taken them almost a full day to traverse the valley, and Alix was beginning to feel the fatigue she had kept at bay so far begin to push through to take hold of her. When she stumbled for a second time, she found it was almost too hard to stand back up. Beag had to reach down and, with surprising gentleness, lifted her to her feet once again. "We are almost there", he said softly, patiently. "Hold out until the top, you will be allowed to rest there". *Rest in her grave*, she thought, remembering Mort's earlier words, but she bit her tongue and allowed the shorter Fae to guide her the last few metres and past the thick walls of the fortress. Whatever awaited her, she would face it on her feet.

Chapter 6

Alix and her escorts were met by a troop of similarly armoured warriors, clad in hardened leathers, they all carried hand-length blades at their waists, their chests bare to show off intricate tattoos and markings. Alix noticed that there seemed to be no distinctions made between genders and noticed that among the four newcomers who approached them, it was the women who had the more elaborate designs.

"Dia's greetings, Mort *Fianna*, Beag *Fianna*". Said the lead Fae, Alix had trouble identifying the gender of the speaker, but the diadem the Fae wore at their brow spoke to some sort of authority, they also did not share the red eyes of the warriors, instead it being a deep amber. Mort and Beag both made small bows, Alix noticed a sense of concern in both the warriors, this individual made them, if not concerned, at least tense.

"Bevan *Draoi*," Mort started as he stood straight, "there was no need to meet us-" he was cut off with a raise of the newcomer, Bevan's, arm.

"Where is Kadir? Where is your lord, *Fianna*?" Bevan asked. Both warriors stiffened at the question, and Mort looked to Beag first before answering.

"*Draoi*, respect, but this may be something we need to discuss with the court", Mort replied, bowing again, deeper this time, seemingly concerned by this mystery figure's reaction. Bevan's response was to simply clasp their arms and bow their head sadly. "It is as I foretold, Kadir has fallen". They stated. Mort and Beag did not respond, but their silence was affirmation enough.

The warriors to either side of Bevan let out a vicious roar, one falling to their knees, pulling at their hair as they screeched. Alix jumped and practically jumped out of her skin, and would have likely fallen to the ground if the warriors surrounding her had given her enough room to, instead she bounced between them as they wailed. Bevan did not move, and Mort and Beag stood stoic as the troop of warriors displayed their grief openly and loudly for all to see. The noise made Alix's blood run cold, but she managed to stay on her feet, head downward, hoping the grieving Fae did not notice her and did not wonder why she was there with the two warriors, tied in bondage between them.

"Enough," Bevan decried, their voice softer but cold as stone, and as one, the warriors regained their composure, no sign of the outpouring of emotion that had just occurred beyond the red rims of their now hard, red eyes. "This is she", she continued, and Alix got the terrifying realisation that Bevan was referring to her. Mort grunted his confirmation, and Bevan stood aside, gesturing up the pathway.

"Then lead on, *Fianna*, our *Tiarna* awaits". *Tiarna? Fianna? Draoi?* Alix thought to herself, what did any of this mean? Why were these people, if they were people and not demons, doing this?

Mort led into the courtyard, the slope of the road rising to bring them onto a plateau of short-manicured grass, shrubs and ferns of odd hues of green and red dotting the green in small decorative bunches. The courtyard was a flurry of activity as Fae, some clearly warriors, their red eyes shining, others having the soft amber like Bevan, walked briskly through, eagerly completing whatever tasks this *Tiarna* had assigned them. A path of large granite stones led from the courtyard up to a larger stone structure nestled up against the sheer cliff face of the mountain. It was long and rectangular in shape and was the largest building Alix had ever seen. She was shocked that something, even of stone, could remain standing while being so large.

Mort and Beag led her towards that building, the troop accompanying Bevan following close behind like honour guards. The large doors at the front of the building were already swung wide open, and lively music flowed out into the courtyard, braziers lit within, pushing back the long shadows of twilight as they stretched toward the entrance. Alix's knees once again became shaky, her bruised and beaten body struggling now to keep her upright and leaving her forced to lean on Beag, who now walked beside her, gently pushing her towards the door, a maw set to swallow her whole and leave nothing left.

Stepping through, she came into a large, well-lit hall, Fae bounded from wall to wall, dancing in beat with the music played by a group of long-haired Fae that sat together at a central table. They played instruments of string and banged drums of hide stretched over wooden hoops. Several of the Fae had thin flutes to their lips, the tune decidedly merry. Bevan, following behind Alix now being harassed by the laughing Fae who pounced at her and threw food and trinkets as the armed procession made its way through the debauchery. Alix could only stand wide eyed staring at the floor as wet pieces of meat and cake slapped off her and the raised shields of the armed guards. Bevan seemed annoyed though did not move to stop them, instead, she strode ahead and gestured the group to follow as she led them further through the hall and past the rambunctious Fae, who shouted and cajoled as they bounced around the hall in each other's arms.

The crowd parted for Bevan, seemingly without noticing her, yet she did not pause in her brisk walk, and always there was space in front of her. They came to yet another large carved door, flanked by angry-looking red-eyed Fae, blades in hand, who Bevan came to a stop in front of. She shared a quick word with one of them, who then slipped through the door, and after a brief moment, Alix stood awkwardly among the joyous music and laughter before the Fae returned and then led the party through.

They were now in a smaller but still large room. Windows set high in the walls allowed what little light remained to illuminate a semi-circular chamber, three wicker chairs arrayed to face the door, all empty, while a group of Fae dressed in the white tunics that seemed the common dress stood in a huddle behind. There was no music in this room, and as the guard stepped back out of the room, closing the door behind her, the silence engulfed them.

Bevan moved to join the group at the back, and Mort and Beag pulled Alix into the centre of the room, Mort roughly pushing her to her knees before cutting her bonds and retreating several steps until both he and Beag had their backs to the door. Alix, alone, now tried to control her breathing, she had made it this far and was not yet dead, maybe she would make it further. She picked nervously at her fingers and ran her eyes across the group, whispering in hushed voices. Bevan was speaking to a broad-shouldered Fae, back to her, he stood taller than most she had seen so far, and though he wore his hair long and wore the white tunic, deep black ink was visible through the fabric, winding images of vines with accompanying sprouting flowers climbed his back, there were the small bulbs of rosemary, wide hands of lilies, intermixed with an odd bulb-like flower, petals layered in a way that seemed to form itself into a heart shape of five petals, thorns running down its stem where it joined the rest of the assembled vines and flowers, the whole illustration seeming to blow in an invisible wind as the Fae tensed, his shoulders raising as he listened to Bevan. Maybe it was the fear, maybe it was the simple alien nature of this place, but she found herself studying that back. All the markings she had seen of these Fae so far were images of violence, of achievement. Why did this one have images of such beauty and calmness?

The tall, stoic Fae did not seem to respond to whatever it was Bevan was saying instead, a beautiful Fae woman, her golden hair braided over one shoulder, stepped forward and whispered harshly to Bevan, pointing a long-nailed finger, lacquered up until the second knuckle with a deep blue dye and poked several times at Bevan's bare chest, seemingly punctuating her unheard words. Bevan took the abuse wordlessly, and Alix wondered if the nail would draw blood before yet another Fae, this one red-eyed and vicious-looking, snarled at the blue nailed Fae, the woman crossing her arms and stepping back. "Enough," the red-eyed Fae barked. "We begin".

The three Fae then turned to look at her, and Alix got her first glimpse of the tall Fae who had tattoos so different from the ones she had seen. His eyes stood out, a simple dark green, yet there was a depth to them, an intelligence within that frightened her. As he gazed at her, she felt as if he could look through her and uncover all her secrets. His face was long like the rest of the Fae, though square-jawed, while the others were pointed. His mouth was flat, but his lips full, a subtle pink that made her think of the berries of the gorse bush that grew along the ridges of her village, his brow powerful, and though he extruded strength, there was a gentleness in how he walked, following the rest of the Fae as he gently lowered himself into the left-handed seat.

The blue lacquered Fae woman was sharp where he had been soft, her eyes, the same amber as the others, were cutting but beautiful, full and inquisitive. She would know Alix's secrets too, but finding out about them would be much less enjoyable, they said, at least for Alix. Her pointed chin sat above a long, elegant neck. Full heart-shaped lips pulled into a disapproving sneer as she looked over the kneeling human. She seemed to almost float as she moved to the wicker chair on the right, sitting and adjusting her tunic to display long noble legs, tight with muscles that were matched by the thin but reinforced shape of her arms, ending in a mass of shoulders that held up the tunic she wore, longer and somehow finer than the rest she had seen.

The final Fae was all power, whereas the others, too, had been subtle. His muscles bulged against the fabric of his tunic, deep black ink covering him from head to toe, an ugly decapitated head, blood dripping from its mouth, sitting proudly upon his brow above deep red eyes that stared at her hungrily. His teeth were bared, twin sets of canines seeming to catch the light from the high-up windows as he bounded into his seat, leaning forward to study her. He was the only one armed of the three, having two blades at his waist, his right hand toying with one as Bevan came to stand at his shoulder.

The red-eyed Fae nodded to no one in particular, and Bevan strode forward to stand before Alix. "Mort *Fianna*, you bring this human to the court. Why?" she intoned.

Mort took a step from the wall to stand behind Alix, "I bring you lord Kadir's killer". He said loudly. "To present to my court and *Tiarna* for them to do as they wish. She was the property of lord Kadir before his death, and as such, the Bronan's laws are clear, she is property now of the court". He bowed low and stepped back to the wall.

"Tell me, Mort *Fianna*, how is it a human, vermin of no use, can kill the lord of the hunt?" sneered the red-eyed Fae. Mort bent low again to answer, "Aodh, my *Tiarna*, I am loyal to you always and will speak truth, this human followed Kadir from its village and set upon him and the *Sluagh* while we searched for better hunting grounds, as lord Kadir had commanded". This time, he did not rise from his position. So the red-eyed one was the *Tiarna*, their leader, Alix supposed. The red-eyed Fae - Aodh - laughed a grim bark at Mort's words.

"My first brother could not be taken by prey. You mock me and this court, Mort, I shall have your entrails for super!" he growled. Mort's face grew pale, but he still did not rise or respond.

Bevan instead turned to Beag, "Beag *Fianna*, is what your companion says true?" Alix was confused. Of course, it was, and Bevan knew that they had just discussed this before entering the chamber, why the formality why continue with this charade, just punish her or don't. Beag strode up to stand beside Mort, bending equally low as he responded.

"It is Bevan *Draoi*, this human managed to damage several *Sluagh* and release several captured thralls before being confronted, bravely," he added quickly, "by lord Kadir, who heroically fought the human before being killed". Beag then began to rummage at the satchel at his waist.

"The human ended lord Kadir with this," he said, pulling forth the horn Alix had last seen jutting from the neck of Kadir as he lay bleeding upon the grass. The sight of it shocked Alix, and a noise came from her throat before she could stop herself. "The thrall recognises the weapon, it seems", crooned the woman to Aodh's right. "Bring it to me, Beag". She commanded.

Once Beag had handed it over, she turned it in her hands, running blue-dyed fingers over the tacky blood that still coated the horn fully. She raised it to her lips and tasted it, running a long tongue over her finger, savouring the taste before smiling and turning to Aodh. "it is our brother's blood, Aodh, I have tasted it enough times to know its foul bite". She spit on the floor before passing the horn to Aodh, who looked over the horn once before offering it to the silent fae man to his left. He refused it, and so Aodh held the horn in his lap as he turned back to the still-bent warriors.

"So my brother was slain by prey with a piece of another prey beast, the lord of the hunt, truly killed by his quarry". He threw his head back in laughter, "how delightfully ironic", he continued. "Did my brother die well, my *Fianna*?" he asked, and Beag looked to Mort before either answered.

"I take it from your silence", began Bevan, "that you cannot find the words to describe correctly the glory in which lord Kadir fell". She finished. Mort was quick to jump on the offered lifeline, "Yes, *Draoi*, indeed, his excellence could not be matched by words spoken by those as insignificant as us". Aodh let out another booming laugh before standing to his feet, "Begone my *Fianna*, spread the tales of this hunt to the people, let us rejoice and be merry at its conclusion, and we will share wine over the memory of my beloved and special brother". He finished with a sneer and chuckled as he turned to the woman at his right.

"Brigit, I give this human to you, you may do with it as you wish". Was all he said as he strode towards the doors, which had opened to allow the scuttling warriors to depart their master's presence.

Brigit bounded to her feet and began to approach Alix, "It is only fair that blood is traded for blood, I shall taste this one, in our brother's memory, of course". She licked her lips as she bent, pulling back Alix's head to stare into her eyes. Alix's breath came fast and ragged now, images of the puddle of blood and mud that had been all that remained of the girl Kadir had killed flashing in her mind.

"That is against our ways", came a quiet but forceful voice. "No human may be consumed within this valley, that is the creed we have made with them". It was the Fae with the flower tattoos. "You cannot kill one we have bound in servitude, Brigit". He said. There was no heat in his voice, no anger, simply stating the facts as they were. Brigit whirled on the still-seated Fae and roared ferociously at him.

"Now, second brother, you wish to speak? Do you question our *Tiarna's* order?" she barked, daring the other Fae to respond.

"I do not, but I remind you of our customs". The soft spoken Fae continued. "She is not to be killed". He stated. Brigit laughed a bitter tune as she whirled to Aodh, now standing at the door, watching the exchange enthusiastically, "See brother," Brigit said, "he calls it she, how smitten our second brother is with his prey". She turned again to Brigit, "Brother, you would not deny me this indulgence, not for one who harmed this court so". She ran her lacquered nails over Alix's neck, and she whimpered pathetically, terrified at the hunger and desperation in Brigit's eyes as she gazed down at her. "Please," was all she was able to manage, sobs beginning to rise in her chest as the fate before her began to be made clear.

The stoic Fae stood now, taking an involuntary step towards the two women before looking at and addressing Aodh. "I am not the second brother any longer, Kadir is dead, Aodh. I am the first brother, and by rights, his property is mine, not Brigit's". Brigit's head swung up then, glaring at the still unnamed Fae, Alix stared too, who was this Fae, what awful terrible deeds would he do to her, or have her do.

Aodh studied them all carefully before a slow smile crept over his face. "Indeed you are Fiachra. You are, of course, right, sorry Brigit, you may not kill this human, it appears that it is to be our sec- first brother's," he corrected himself, "plaything". He turned to Alix then, "You may wish for Brigit's bite before he is done with you," he said, and seeing the fear and confusion on Alix's face, he turned once again and, with a laugh, bounded out to join the music and dance.

Brigit gave her brother, Fiachra, one final look before too bounding out after the others. Leaving Alix alone with her would be savior, maybe she would end up regretting the missed opportunity of a quick death.

Chapter 7

Alix stared at Fiachra as the tall, wide-shouldered Fae watched his retreating compatriots. She could see tightness in his eyes and began to worry that maybe Aodh's warning was right. Maybe this Fae could be just as bad as the others, maybe even worse.

"Wait here," he said before he turned and strode from the room, slamming the large oak doors shut behind him. Alix, alone now in the chambers, rose to her feet unsurely, looking around at her surroundings. Not for an exit, it had been clear since they entered the valley that escape was not as simple as getting out into the open air, but rather to take in the alien nature of this new world, a world she may be resigned to spending the rest of her life in. A life that appeared to be growing shorter and shorter by the second. She glanced around the room quickly looking to see if there was anything heavy or sharp enough to defend herself with, but judging by how Kadir had held up against her arrows it was unlikely anything here would strike a killing blow. It was even more unlikely that she would just find another magik horn lying about.

Beyond the chairs, nestled in the alcove at the back of the chamber, stood a simple birch table draped in a fine green and gold rug. It held many small objects on it, pieces of bone carved with faces, and rope that seemed to be made of spun gold. Alix stepped closer to the table and gasped, spotting the horn. It was still caked in blood, tossed uncaringly on top, as if this Fae was unconcerned leaving her alone with a weapon that was capable of killing their kind. She let out a quiet laugh of disbelief, and her fingers twitched as she stared at the weapon. But something stopped her from rushing forward and grabbing it. First of all, she thought, where would she have hidden such a large object? Her clothes, torn and ragged from the drama of the past few days, barely hid her nakedness. She would be hard-pressed to hide a shining blue horn over a foot in length as well.

Instead, she focused on the artwork, hoping that when the Fae returned he would forget the horn so she could think of somewhere safe to stash it. She moved closer to admire the large frescos that covered the back of the chamber. Unlike most of the carvings she had seen decorating the homes and buildings of the Fae, this art was a burst of colour. Hues of all shades danced as beautifully designed spirals seemed to morph together, displaying an idealised version of the valley, showing the wheat fields and villages that made up the lower part, rising to the palace and tower, overlooking the valley, sunlight shining from behind as if the palace itself was the source of all light. She reached out to run her hand along the fine lines that seemed to come together at the valley edge, when a sound caused her to jump.

Fiachra reentered the enclosed chamber and stopped as he saw her standing at the chamber's rear. He seemed startled to see her on her feet, and for a moment, she thought she saw the hint of a smirk touch his lips. Behind him, carrying a white cloth bundle, came a human, collared with eyes downcast, she stood a head shorter than Fiachra, her black hair worn tight in a short ponytail. Her eyes were green and held the same timidness that every human seemed to have here, a placidness that terrified Alix in a way she couldn't explain.

"This is Aine", Fiachra said, gesturing to the demure woman at his side. "She is the head maid and will get you acquainted with your roles and duties here". He said. He reached within the bundle of cloth and pulled a silver worked collar from the parcel. Alix stiffened and took an involuntary step back. Fiachra, for his part, noticed her unease and did not

71

attempt to approach her. He held the silver collar in his hands and looked at her almost apologetically. "If you are to stay here, you must wear a collar. The house thralls wear collars of silver to show their treasured place in our halls. All must wear them". Aine sure enough, head still lowered but green eyes watching her fiercely now, wore a matching silver collar, seemingly made from silver somehow weaved together in a way that was both delicate and displayed a certain sturdiness that Alix felt would make the collars look unbreakable.

"I am not your slave", Alix spat, and she was proud of how little her voice shook. It did certainly shake, but not as much as she would have thought, given the situation. Fiachra looked down at the collar, toying with it in his hands for a moment and seemed to struggle with what to say. "I am sorry, but, unfortunately... you are". That was what he eventually decided to say. Alix took another step back, her hips hitting the oak table, shaking all the items placed upon it, rolling the dark blue horn to knock against her hand.

Fiachra's eyes shot to the horn, his muscles seeming to bulge in anticipation, but he did not move towards her. "Aine, please leave us and ready our new maid's bedding, leave the dress behind". Aine's green eyes flashed from the tall Fae to Alix and back again, a pleading in her eyes as if to ask Alix not to do anything stupid in her absence before gently placing the folded white fabric at her feet and retreating through the oak doors.

Fiachra and Alix locked eyes, and Alix could sense her body tense with determination, with her will to survive. Her limbs felt cold and tingly as the horn seemed to call to her, commanding her to take it up. She resisted the urge to grab it, to even look at it, for fear of attracting more attention to it before she could hide it. Fiachra did not move from his spot but instead raised his arms to either side, the movement causing the fabric of his dress to slip from one shoulder, revealing more of his bodywork of vines and flowers, powerful muscles moving underneath. It was meant to be a disarming action, Alix was sure, but the simple size difference between the two of them made any such attempt at persuasion seem hollow. This Fae could rip her in half without straining himself, and they both knew it.

As Alix shuffled further away, he did not follow but instead spoke. "Did you lose anyone?" he asked, and Alix was shocked at the earnestness in his voice. She did not speak, not sure how to answer such a question from him. "When my brother attacked?" he clarified, as if there could have been any confusion as to what recent dramatic event he could be referring too. Alix blinked a few times before answering, stunned and unsure of what to say other than the truth. "Yes. My cousins, I think". She said, "though someone said that they might have seen them running off into the forest.", she added. "He killed someone special to me, your brother." She whispered. "He killed Keemre". Fiachra nodded solemnly. "I am sorry", he said, and again, Alix was caught off guard by the emotion behind the words. Anger replaced fear as she snapped "I don't care!", enraged at his attempt at sympathy for the brutal violence his kind had wrought on her clann, "You monsters did it, who gives a *fuck* about your sorry?" She didn't realise she was screaming until the words had already left her, the fear of angering this odd demi-god lost in her anger. "He killed Keemre, and then he killed and ate a poor child, you are all monsters, and I hate you all!" and she sneered, "I will kill all of you!".

Fiachra waited a moment, watching Alix who was now breathing heavily and tense with unreleased fury. He moved cautiously in his seat before responding. "Who was Keemre?" he asked.

Alix spat at him, a wad of saliva covering the metres between them and landing grossly on his dress. She had an instant fear of retaliation, but Fiachra just brushed it off and asked again, "Was she your mother?"

"No," Alix responded, backing up further until she had reached the edge of the table and began to move around it, "She was our clann's wise woman. She took me in as a baby". She continued, refusing to allow Fiachra's attempt at connection."In my culture, anyone who cares for a child can claim ownership of it", he said.

Alix laughed, "Keemre did not own me, no one can own a person". Fiachra nodded apologetically, "Of course, I apologise, I meant only that she was important to you. My brother took her from you, and though my apology cannot mean much, I offer it to you. My mother was also taken from me. It is not an easy loss to endure".

Slowly, Fiachra lowered himself to the stone floor of the chamber. Hands still raised, silver collar still grasped in one. "What is your name?" he asked. Alix thought to withhold it for a second, refusing to give her name as a sign of defiance but ultimately decided to. "Alix", she growled. "Alix," he repeated, running his mouth over the name a few times as he got the pronunciation correct. "Alix, you are captured and unfortunately taken to our land. By laws stronger than me, you are a thrall". His voice was still soft, full of understanding and apologetic in a way that made Alix's blood rise again.

"You want to fight, to lash out, to go down fighting with our blood in your mouth. I know, I can see it in you. If you truly wish that I will not stop you, I will bear my throat to you if you but ask, but then you will be at the mercy of my kin, and I do not wish that on anyone, let alone a helpless human". He toyed again with the collar in his hands before opening it and placing it around his own neck. It snapped shut, and he smiled at Alix. "Just because you must look a certain way does not make it true". He pulled at a piece of the collar, and it snapped open again. "If you wear a collar, you are no more captive than you allow yourself to be". He slipped it off his neck and offered it towards Alix. "I can show you how to remove it, so you only need to wear it when performing your duties, I will not ask of you any more than that".

Alix did not approach the Fae. Instead, she remained where she stood, puzzled. She felt almost dizzy from the whiplash of emotions. After a moment, Fiachra, smiling softly, placed the collar down on top of the dress. "If you change your mind, I will leave these here. Aine will be waiting for you outside. I ask you not to take that horn with you as my sister will notice it missing, she hated Kadir more than most and is likely hoping to keep that as a souvenir". He rose, empty handed and moved towards the door. "I am very sorry for what has happened to you and your people Alix. It is awful and terrible". And with that, he stepped out once again.

As soon as the door shut, Alix buckled to the ground, she kept her eyes on the door, but as the minutes passed and no one entered, the sobs returned, and she pulled her knees to her chest as they took over. As they subsided, Alix was left red-faced and once again embarrassed at her lack of control over her emotions. A memory of Keemre appeared in her mind. She was smiling softly at her, soothing the pain away from some long-forgotten injury, and the tears threatened to return. Rubbing the tears away before they had a chance to fall, she pushed herself to her feet and walked over to the slight pile of white fabric.

Looking over the white dress, she felt her cheeks heat at the sheerness of the fabric, even folded her hand seemed to be almost visible through the dress. She placed the collar to the side for the moment and quickly pulled her ruined shirt over her head. She dressed quickly and was thankful the palace was well heated, lest she be even more mortified than she was already. Now came the hard part. She picked up the silver collar and turned it over in her hands. It was intricate, beautiful even. If it wasn't what it was, it would have made a pretty piece. Thin strands of silver wrapped around themselves, interlaced with spirals and swirls, like waves running through the metal across its entire length. She could not see the latch or mechanism Fiachra had used to open the collar. She tested it a few times and was confused when It didn't seem to lock, and trying a few times, she wondered if it was broken. She raised it to her neck but could go no further. Her hand shook as she held the circlet there.

She took a deep breath, then screamed. She screamed for Keemre, for her cousins, for all the pain and destruction and violence. She screamed for the dead, those she knew the names of and those she didn't. She screamed for the little girl, for what had happened to her, she screamed for what Kadir had done, what he had made her do to him. She screamed for her situation, and she didn't stop until she sat kneeling on the ground, out of breath. Then, picking the collar back up, she placed it to her neck and closed it without allowing herself to think on it for much longer, hearing the collar finally click as it closed in place, snug to her neck. She let out a sob. Forcing herself to calm, she took a long breath and found she could still breathe without discomfort. Taking another, she touched it, running her finger across the collar. Fiachra's neck was so broad and wide, how had the collar seemed to fit him? She wondered. Before deciding that, like most questions here, the answer was better left unsaid.

Smoothing her dress, breathing slowly and intentionally, willing herself to be calm, she finally approached the door. She looked one last time at the horn, failing to think of any way she might be able to stash it on her person. She let herself believe there must be another way for her to fight back, mentally letting go of the horn and stepping towards the door. Slowly, she pulled it open and stepped through. Aine was indeed standing there waiting for her. Judging by the concerned light in her green eyes, Alix's outbursts had not gone unnoticed, but Aine had the good graces to not ask any questions.

"Follow me", was all she said before turning and moving in a well practised motion through the now thick crowd of rowdy Fae. Alix made her best effort to follow, dodging Fae as they danced wildly through the crowd, flagons of wine splashing red liquid through the air as the musicians played a rowdy beat. As Aine moved past an especially rowdy table of red-eyed Fae, two of them fell between the shuffling humans. Alix started at the violence as the female Fae squirmed on top of the larger male Fae, momentarily shocked at the power on display before Aine, now at her shoulder, firmly pulled her along. "First rule, do not stare, especially at the *Fianna*". She said in hushed tones as she pulled Alix along.

"Why were they fighting?" Alix responded as Aine let out a low, dull laugh. "How young are you, child? They were not fighting". Alix's cheeks flushed again. She would need to get a handle on that eventually before responding gruffly to Aine. "I am not a child," she muttered, wincing at the familiarity of the word that the wise women of her clann would use so affectionately with her, that Keemre used with her. "What are the *Fianna*?" she asked instead, changing the subject from the rutting Fae. Aine shook her head in response as she pulled Alix through the final part of the hall and out into the courtyard.

The sun had now set completely, and white-robed thralls walked the length of the courtyard, lighting torches set into carved alcoves along the walls, each one designed in such a way so that the flame seemed to illuminate carved faces, each one seeming to display an exaggerated relief of emotion, one consumed by anguish, another by bliss. Alix continued to be pulled as Aine made her way across the courtyard and towards a separate, less-ordained hall at the base of the large tower. Only inside did Aine finally let go of her, allowing Alix a moment to fix her dress, reminding herself again of the thinness of the fabric. She opened her mouth to speak, but Aine spoke first.

"You have a lot of questions, I know, we all did at first, but you must know some basics before then. First and most important is that you are a thrall, that is a fact, yes it is uncomfortable, no, none of us are happy about it, but it is what it is, we survive and continue," she paused a moment her green eyes searching Alix's for a moment, seeking if the truth had hit home before continuing. "You cannot say no to anything, child. We are lucky that the Fae must abide by rules, so you will not be asked to bed any of them, though some may try, though as Lord Fiachra is to take you into his… *personal* service, I doubt any would wish to dishonour him to try".

Dishonour him, not her, Alix noted. Aine seemed to notice the annoyance and snapped her fingers to grab Alix's attention, "Lord Fiachra is a good one, Alix, you are lucky, though I understand it doesn't feel like it right now". She gestured for Alix to follow her down a cramped hallway, wall to wall, with small doors, some open showing cramped quarters, each with a pair of bunk beds in each room.

"You will have your own bed and a trunk, several dresses which will be cleaned for you so you won't have to worry about that," Aine stopped at an open door, turning to face Alix. "this is going to be hard girl", she said her green eyes hard as she stared down Alix. "But you are choosing to survive, that cannot be taken from you. Hold onto that, no one can take that from you". She nodded, then to one of the beds. "This is yours, try and rest, I have asked your dormmates to give you space tonight, but don't expect that sort of luxury going forward. And please, girl, do not try and escape tonight the *Fianna* are in a sort, and I'd rather not have to bury what remains of you tomorrow". Alix nodded slowly before looking over the small room. A tiny window sat across from the door, and between that and the cramped beds, there was room for little else.

"I must leave you now, girl, but I will be back for you in the morning. I don't know how early you rose before, but if you aren't used to an early start yet, best start getting used to it". She gently pushed Alix into the tiny room, pointing again at the lower bunk on the left. "Sleep", she said before closing the door behind her. Alix's body seemed to decide for her what came next, and giving in, she lay down on the bed, her bed, and closed her eyes, allowing the darkness to take her.

***

Alix woke with a start, sitting up fast enough to bash her head into the frame above. She lay back, cradling her head as the memories of the night before came rushing back. She turned to the other pair of beds and noticed the huddled shapes of others, fast asleep despite the loud crack her head had made against the bed above. She lay there for a while, watching the window as the night outside began to lighten. This was how Aine found her when she came for her.

"Ah, you're awake, good", she began, tossing Alix a fresh dress, "Hurry girl, we have no time for modesty, dress and meet me at the door". With that, she turned and moved back down the hall.

Alix quickly pulled the fresh dress over her body, again blushing as the thin fabric brushed against her skin, the cold morning wind feeling harsh against her skin. Barefooted, she walked down the hallway, dodging similarly dressed thralls as they, too, started their morning before emerging out into the still dark morning. Aine was there waiting, watching as the thralls rushed around the large courtyard. Alix allowed herself to watch as they bustled. Some carried large crates into the palace hall, some were busy weeding and watering plants within the courtyard, and many more seemed to scurry like ants, each to their tasks.

Aine spotted her then and approached, stuffing a large piece of bread and accompanying slab of cheese into her hands before motioning to eat. Alix obliged, suddenly aware of how hungry she was and quickly stuffed the food into her mouth. Aine began moving across the yard towards the palace hall, and Alix followed, finishing the bread and cheese before they crossed the threshold.

Within the hall, many thralls were already busy cleaning the floors and walls of wine and other stains that had appeared overnight. A pile of sleeping Fae, all in a varied state of undress, lay at the end of one of the large tables, the thralls cleaning around them, careful not to disturb them. Alix initially thought that she would join them, but Aine led her past them and towards an open hallway that ran down, descending into the mountain itself. She paused momentarily before following Aine as she moved down the hallway.

They passed several more halls and rooms, each one shocking her at the size of the palace as it seemed to continue on and on. She became uncomfortable, aware of the mountain above them as they went. Shockingly, it was not cold or damp like she thought, the light coming from the torches seeming to be brighter than it should have any right to be. "It's magik", Aine said, "best not to think how they do it", sensing Alix's anxiety. "No." Alix said, stopping in place. "What the fuck is this place Aine". The other woman sighed angrily and pulled Alix to the side of the corridor. "You are going to need to get a grip of yourself, and quickly, Alix. You work and live for their pleasure not your own. If you make a mistake, even a small one, you will get punished. If you make the mistake again, the punishment will be worse, Alix.

"Your friends, your family, they will all be targeted if you do not perform. Especially if it looks like it is intentional. Please, for all our sakes, be smart".

They continued past yet another large room, and several Fae, including Brigit, Alix noticed, eating a meal of meats and vegetables of all kinds in quantities that made Alix's eyes widen before they came to a seemingly small, unordained door. Aine opened it and gestured for Alix to enter. She did, and as the door closed behind her, the noise from outside ceased.

In the sudden silence, Alix felt unsure of herself. She looked to Aine, who gestured and continued down the hall. "This is Lord Fiachra's private chambers. You will spend most of your time here, cleaning, fetching, whatever it is he needs from you, you will do, They emerged out into a large room, a fireplace sat blazing set within one wall and opposed a large window was cut into the stone, a magnificent view of the valley stretched as far as she could see. From here, it seemed the entire valley was visible.

Alix approached the window slowly, feeling the wind hit her as she did. "How…" she attempted, but words escaped her. "Lord Fiachra keeps himself separate from the others, and he built this refuge as far as he could from the rest of them while still under the mountain. He will claim it is for the view, but I think it is because he just does not like his kin". The sound of a door opening turned both their heads, and Aine, clasping her hands in front of her, bent her head as Fiachra approached. He wore only a loincloth of similar fabric to Alix's dress, and Alix adverted her eyes as his manhood was evident through the sheer fabric.

"Good morning, Lord", Aine said, shooting a critical eye to Alix, who had now wore a look of defiance and contempt on her face. He nodded his response before walking past them, either he was oblivious to Alix or was choosing to ignore her scowl. Without a word, he sat upon a white fur pillow and turned to stare out the window. The ink upon his back seemed to ripple as he leaned back to rest on his hands, his unbound hair blowing in the wind that came barreling through the large set window.

Aine elbowed Alix, getting her attention before gesturing towards the door Fiachra had just vacated. They left the Fae to his quiet, and Alix begrudgingly followed Aine through the doorway. They entered a large room, a large bed, covered with fur rugs of many different animals, some of which Alix recognised, though many she did not.

Aine began to pull them, forming them into some sort of order before turning annoyed green eyes on Alix. "I am not doing this myself, girl. These are your duties, don't forget". Sufficiently chastised, Alix moved to join Aine. After all, it was not her fault that this had become her life. After they had organised the bed, they gathered the discarded clothes. They continued with the room before emerging, hands full with bedding and clothes, back into the main room of the chamber. Fiachra sat where they had left him, still staring out over the valley. Once they were done with the bedroom, Aine led her out of Fiachra's chambers to a separate laundry room filled with hard-working thralls, where they deposited the bedding. Alix took a seat, brushing the sweat from her brow, the thin garment now seeming to make a lot more sense before Aine pulled her back to her feet. "Not done yet", she chuckled as she pushed a large pail of water into one hand and a thick cloth into the other.

They returned and set about scrubbing the floors of the large private chambers. Fiachra, for his part, ignored them, content to sit and stare out over the valley, seemingly oblivious to them as they toiled. After several trips to empty the dirty water, refill the pails and start again, Alix could feel her blood boil. She had done housework before, of course, but never for so long.

It was undignified, the Fae man who had tried to coax her gently into the collar she now wore seemed to not even notice her. By the time the apartments were cleaned spotless, the mid-day sun shone bright overhead, and Alix's breath laboured, partly from the exertion, partly from rage.

"Anything else, my lord?" Aine asked as she brushed wrinkled fingers against her shift. Fiachra did not turn, of course, so busy he was with watching over his domain and simply waved a hand in dismissal. Aine turned to go, but Alix had had enough.

"No",. she said, and Aine flinched at the acid in her voice. "You made me a promise, Fae" She spurted out before she could stop herself, a hiss from Aine telling her it was the absolute wrong thing to say.

But, it got Fiachra's attention. The stoic Fae turned lazily to finally look at her, and her heart skipped a beat as those green eyes pierced hers. She again got a sense that he could see all of her, know all her secrets and desires through those golden brown eyes. It made her skin crawl, and she suppressed a shiver, intent on not letting his gaze dissuade her from her task.

"Indeed". He said after a pregnant moment, "You may leave, Aine". He said. Aine paused only a moment, shooting a look that promised words later before shuffling away. Fiachra waited until they heard the soft click of the door closing behind her before speaking.

"I am sorry, I was distracted. I had not noticed you". He said. "If that is an apology, it is a sorry one". She replied.

Thankful that the nerves that seemed ready to shake her silly managed to stay from her voice.

"Yes, you are right". That was all he said. Standing now and stretching, Alix made sure to keep her eyes locked on his, making sure that her eyes did not wander over his muscular chest, the single loincloth slightly ajar, showing more skin than a man should feel comfortable showing to a woman.

"You wish to know how to remove the collar?" he asked as he strode across the room, bending to pick a small wooden cup from a low table and pouring himself a drink from an accompanying gourd. He reached for a second cup and poured another, placing it on the table and gesturing for her to join him.

"Just tell me how to take this thing off". She said, not moving from her spot, arms crossed under her breasts. Fiachra nodded quickly, taking a quick swig from his cup before walking over to her and placing his hand gently around her neck. She jumped at the touch, her eyes going wide as his long fingers wrapped around her neck, gently pulling her forward.

His strength was evident in the motion, and she felt suddenly aware of the difference in power between them. All he had to do was squeeze, and she was sure her head would simply pop, but he didn't, instead, his thumb traced the line of the collar, searching along her neck before resting under her chin. He gently lifted it, and she found herself staring into his eyes once more. He smiled apologetically before turning his gaze to her neck. His thumb seemed to snag on something, and with a click, the collar came loose, clattering to the floor at her feet. Despite herself, she took a shaky inhale, hands going to her neck as soon as the collar was free. They ended up resting on his hand, still gently but firmly around her throat, and at her touch, he flinched and carefully removed his hand.

Their eyes met again, and she saw something new there, a curiosity quickly repressed before he turned and quickly returned to his spot at the window. "There is a latch under the oak leaf, push down on it, and it should come away easy. If you cannot find it, I can show you again". He did not look at her again, and a part of her was irked at that, her own curiosity wanting to see what else hid within those eyes, but she caught herself, reminding herself just who he was, what he was.

Picking the collar of the ground, she inspected it, finding the latch Fiachra had mentioned, she carefully clicked it back around her neck. She toyed with the latch for a few seconds, trying to replicate the action Fiachra had done and then suddenly, click, and she was free again. She sighed with relief, a feeling she had not felt since arriving in the valley, and caught Fiachra watching her again. He turned as soon as her eyes found his and blushed, remembering Aine's waning about some Fae.

"Thank you". She said begrudgingly. He nodded his acknowledgement, eyes fixed on the valley below.
"You may go," was all he said in response, and so she did, passing out through the door and back the long climb to the grand entrance hall and into the courtyard. Her body was warm, but she told herself that it was just the day's activities as she moved to the thrall's house, truly exhausted and aching for her bed.

Aine caught her before then, and she indeed had words for her. But, Alix found herself distracted by the additional chores Aine assigned her, penance, she said, for speaking out of turn to the Fae, not angering her as it should. Instead, she thought of the strange interaction with the Fae lord, how he had flinched when she touched him. A monster of such power, it appeared he could lift mountains, somehow afraid of her touch. That contradictory fact confused her, and as she returned to the thrall house, exhausted like had never been before, she dreamt of a monster who ran from her.

Chapter 8

Alix's days continued much as the first did. Waking, eating quickly, and then going straight to work. By the third day, she was cleaning Fiachra's apartments by herself, Aine trusting her enough not to spend the time at her shoulder. Then, once those chores were completed, it was on to the rest of the palace. It appeared that being Fiachra's personal thrall did not save her from the vast amount of chores a palace of this size needed to function. She spent the rest of her days scrubbing pots, hand-cleaning floors, dusting portraits and folding endless piles of laundry.

As Aine promised, she came to know her dormmates well, the bustle of the mornings forcing interactions out of necessity as the four women all arose and busied themselves before the chores of the day started. Maeve was Alix's bunkmate, quick to bed and last to rise, she was about Alix's age, brown eyes sitting in a sullen face, she was the most recent captive beside Alix at the palace. Her hourglass figure hugged the thin fabric of her dress, and it seemed the attention that gained her from some of their fellow thralls had begun to eat away at her, that was until the other two women in their dorm interfered.

Nora and Tallulah were alike enough that they appeared twins if not for the colour of their skin, Nora was fair, while Tallulah was a darker brown. Their black hair was streaked with grey and while Nora had been at the palace longest, Tallulah was only behind her a few months. Nora came from the Frost Isles and was taken by a raiding party that had landed ashore near her village while she was a child. She did not remember much of her former life, though the still knew a few old Frost Isle curses she liked to throw out on occasion. When she did, she was always very apologetic that she did not know the full meaning of the words. Even the simplest aspects of her culture, ripped away from her. Tallulah was from a large nomadic family and had been sold along with her own and other families to the Fae by slavers in the western plains. She rarely talked about her previous life and no one made any attempt to pry.

When Maeve had returned, red-eyed yet again, the two older women had snuck away late at night, only to return giggling to their beds.

Alix had wondered if they had gotten into the wine. Each of them was rationed a cup at dinner, which they ate in the large room at the far back of the barracks, but as daylight broke, their crime became evident. The two men who had seemed to be making sport of Maeve were covered head to toe in red rashes, the two of them shifting uncomfortably in their white tunics. The giggling and pointing from the women and the Fae who noticed seemed to sting more than whatever nettles the women had stuffed their beds full of, and Maeve was left alone after that.

Alix found herself opening her collar and snapping it shut repeatedly, a nervous tick that developed as the days passed Nora caught her doing it one morning and pulled her aside before the day began. "I see you have got the trick of it", she had said, smiling kindly as she did so, "but don't let them see you do that, or you will get yourself in trouble, especially with Ain. She is one of us, but she runs a tighter ship than the *Aos Si*". Nora always used the correct term when referring to the Fae, an odd idiosyncrasy that a few of the thralls seemed to have. Those who did so seemed to have a veneration of the Fae, too. It made Alix uncomfortable and it was clear she was not the only one.

"The devoted". Maeve had told her, "That's what we call them. They are mostly harmless, but if you want to moan about any of the pointy ears, best make sure they are not around. You never know what they tell their bedmates". Alix was shocked at the amount of thralls who went to the bed of their Fae captors. Every night there was a flow of a dozen or so thralls sneaking back into the barracks. Often to the ire of Aine who ensured those not back by curfew spent the next day with their necks deep in pots, scrubbing until their hands and tunics were black with soot and grease. What was noticeable however was that the majority of them were men, Alix made that observation to her new friends one night which induced a fit of laughter from the women.

"Well Alix, men are not as smart as women, they see the tall Fae and all they see are those bare tits. They don't think about what they are attached to". Tallulah explained between giggles, "They don't seem to know what they are in for until it's too late" she added.

Alix was curious now, "like what" she had asked.

"Well I heard", began Nora, "the female *Aos Si* rode those poor men like unbroken mules", she giggled. "I heard," Talulah added, "that they like to bite!" "I heard," Maeve cut in, "that their women play this game with them, they take turns and share one man, making him keep going long after he has found completion!" Alix joined in the laughter then.

Those first few days were surprisingly good. The work was hard but Fiachra did not make any attempt to speak with her again, the nights spent gossiping and laughing with her new friends. She still spent most nights wondering where her family were. Who, if any, of her cousins had survived and where they could be. She began to settle, though uncomfortably, into her new role, that was until she came face to face with Bevan. She had learned that her name was not Bevan *Draoi*, but rather *Draoi* was her title. She was what went for a wise woman for the Fae and could operate with complete impunity. Nora said not even Aodh, the leader of all the Fae within the valley could tell her no. And, as Maeve was more than happy to share, she took advantage of that power frequently, especially late at night.

She had spotted Bevan several times those first few days, the *Draoi* woman seemed to always be where she was working, she would watch her until Alix noticed before seeming to float away out of sight. Her presence always drew eyes, her leather skirt and bare tattooed chest standard fare, same as most Fae, her ornate tiara of polished bone catching everyone's eyes as she entered or left a room.

This time was different. As Alix entered Fiachra's chambers one day, fresh sheets bundled to her chest, she came across a waiting Bevan at the door. Alix came to a sudden halt before bowing her head respectfully and shuffling off towards the bed chamber. Bevan stepped in front of her and pushed a long nailed hand into her chest. Alix stopped in her tracks and took several steps back, Bevan's fingers pressed to her chest as she followed.

"You are the one who killed Kadir", she said as Alix swallowed loudly. "Yes", she responded though Bevan had not said it as a question. "I read his geise, I saw his death many years ago," Bevan continued, Alix's back now pressed to the oak door of Fiachra's apartments. "I will read yours too, Alix Fae-Slayer" She grabbed Alix's chin then and pulled her to her until Alix's nose was a hair's breadth from Bevan's. Her amber eyes had a reddish hue to them she had not noticed until now, a hungry look in her fox-like eyes.

Alix tried to pull back and Bevan's nails bit into her skin, a sound escaped her then and Bevan blinked, stepping back. "Follow", she commanded and strode into the antechamber towards the heart set into the far wall. Alix thought to run, wondering how far she would get before Bevan caught her, what would she do to her if she did. Before following the *Draoi* into the room.

Alix followed the tall Fae woman as she moved to the lush Erlking pillows set into an alcove of the room. The *Draoi* lounged back into the dense pillows, making a show of relaxing, unbothered, queen on her throne. Alix kept her eyes downcast as the Fae lounged seductively, uncaring how her leather skirt bunched, exposing herself to Alix. There was awareness of calculated motion and Alix remembered Maeve's story of Fae women and their captive men.

Bevan smirked at Alix as she noticed the woman shift uncomfortably under her gaze. She lazily twirled her finger slowly and Alix quickly understood the command in the action. She turned slowly, mouth set in a thin line as she could feel the Fae woman's eyes run over her body, up her legs, over her hips apprasingly and Alix smarted at the way the *Draoi* seemed to judge her like nothing more than a piece of meat.

"Enough" she barked and Alix stopped, turning back to face the reposed Fae. She smiled wickedly before growling, "You will do". She bounded to her feet and suddenly was within a hair's breadth of Alix's face. Her eyes seemed to swirl, the amber turning quickly and violently red, forcing Alix to retreat backwards, the Fae woman following in step.

She grabbed Alix by the base of her neck and pulled her close. "Don't move". She warned as her eyes, frantic, searched Alix's, the white quickly turning bloodshot as she stared unblinking into Alix, searching for something. Alix tried to keep her breathing steady but the sight of those large red eyes, the twin canines glistening in her mouth as the Fae seemed to pant in anticipation.

"I can see your geise, thrall, shall I tell it to you" Bevan laughed then, a bitter one, "Oh it is a tasty future you have". Bevan laughed again before suddenly gasping in shock, the fist holding her neck, yanking her head back as the Fae loomed over her, eyes delirious as the long nails tore her skin, causing Alix to yell out in pain.

"Let her go, crone", came a quiet voice that still somehow seemed to fill the room, the voice small yet booming within Alix's skull. Bevan was instantly away from her, stepping bad, a look of barely concealed horror on her face as she watched Alix. Fiachra stepped into the room, his green eyes were hooded and dark as he stared intently at the *Draoi*.

"Fiachra, her geise -" she began but Fiachra roared, the sound reverberating through the room, somehow sending Bevan splashing against the far wall. She hit the carved grey rock with a crunch and fell to a heap on the ground. *Magick*, Alix thought.

"I have warned you, Bevan, that if I found you in my chambers again I would take your head". Bevan struggled to rise. Red blood blooming at her scalp running down thickly across her face. "Fiachra, her geise, I must tell you, tell the court -" Fiachra stood over the prone Fae, driving his foot into her chest, bringing a low hiss from Bevan.

"Are you alright, Alix?" he asked as Alix, shaking at the sight of the two Fae, muscles bulging, eyes wide as they stared, teeth bared at each other, two angry gods about to war.

"Yes", Alix lied, feeling her warm blood drip down her back, staining her thin shift, causing it to stick tacky to her skin. Fiachra grimaced, hearing the lie but deciding not to call her on it.

"Your services are not needed today, return to the barracks", he ordered, eyes still on the cowering Fae beneath him. Without another word, Alix turned and fled the apartment. She was in a daze as she moved briskly through the palace, though most of the Fae, lounging or laughing in small groups seemed not to notice her, every human she passed seemed to stare, each new pair of eyes adding to her humiliation, she felt the tears as they pooled and wiped them away before they had a chance to fall, she would not allow those Fae to see her cry. She refused to show them that.

As she approached the barracks, vision blurry from the tears, someone grabbed her from behind, without thinking she turned and threw a fist, allowing her anger to finally be released, all the rage, the injustice these monsters dealt out without remorse, without any fairness. Her fist met the seemingly rock-hard muscle of Fiachra's midriff, again he flinched, but at her touch or the punch she couldn't tell.

They stood there, both shocked still. A thrall could not, ever, hit a Fae, yet she just did. A moment passed then, throwing away any sense of self-preservation, Alix began pummeling the Tall Fae. Fiachra stood there, taking each punch wordlessly. Tears were now falling freely down her cheeks as she screamed repeatedly "I hate you, I hate you, I hate you!" over and over she battered the Fae until, herself spent she fell to the ground in tears. She felt large hands lift her gently from the ground and carry her into the barracks.

She continued to weep, angry at herself for the tears, angry for Fiachra for carrying her, angry at all Fae for forcing this on her. She was gently laid on her bunk and she heard hushed voices speaking. "Help her, please" came Fiachra's quiet voice. Hushed voices gave their assent then Aine and Nora's soft voices were near her, a damp cloth patting at her neck.

"Shh girl, it is okay we are here". Aine said, stroking her hair as Alix wept silently. "We are right here".

***

Alix awoke late at night, taking a second to adjust to the low light coming in from the full moon out their small window. She lay bare underneath her sheets, her sheer dress removed at some point through the night, a cloth was wrapped around her neck, wadded at the back where Bevan's nails had bitten her. She pushed herself up to her elbows, the blanket falling away as she looked around her room. Her dormmates were all in their bunks, asleep under their duvets. But as Alix scanned the room she noticed one additional occupant that caused her a mild shock. Aine lay asleep on a mound of blankets by the edge of her bed. A small wooden bowl with water and blood stained rag beside her.

She had a moment of shame at their attentiveness, the fact Aine spent her night not in her own bed, but on the cold hard floor of her room before a sense of warmth and gratitude rose for her small pod of friends. How fast they had come to care for her, and she, them. Women trapped in a world not of their own, finding solace and companionship in each other despite their hardship.

She rose then, the blanket wrapped around her as she moved to the hallway and down towards the well and waiting pitchers of fresh spring water. Her ordeal and waterwork from the night before left her dehydrated, a booming ache in her head driving her small frame onward.

As she reached the open door to the barracks she paused as she spotted a familiar back in the moonlight. Fiachra sat on a stump outside the barracks, his wide shoulders bare under the silvery moon. She paused at the exit, remembering her tirade of words and fists the night before. Wondering why the Fae Lord waited outside. Was it for her? To punish? To protect? She could not understand this Fae and his intentions. Nervously she gulped, her dry throat scratchy as she did so, torn between stepping out in search of water and not wanting to catch his gaze, and starting a conversation she did not want to have.

As she stood there indecisive, a distant red glow appeared from the palace doors across the courtyard and she saw Fiachra stiffen, rising from his stump. The simple tunic he wore seemed to somehow fit him like armour, and hands gripped in fists at his waist spoke of unspent strength, waiting for their next victim. Noise soon reached her from the palace as the doors swung open and several red-eyed Fae, Aodh at their head, stormed towards the barracks. Many carried torches, alight as they each carried those wicked long knives in their hands, several of them glistening in the light from their fire, matching the red in their eyes.

Aodh stopped several feet from Fiachra, his chest rising and falling rapidly, muscles straining as he panted, a hunting Fox searching for his prey.

"Move brother", he hissed. "Your lord has business with the thralls". He intoned. Fiachra did not move from his spot, a sentinel standing watch, but he responded with a low quiet boom of a voice that seemed to rebound within her skull.

"No". The accompanying Fae seemed to flinch at the word, several taking an unconscious step back from him, many more raising their knives menacingly, fear and outrage clear behind their hungry red eyes. They had felt that boom too, the magik in Fiachra's voice both forceful and furious.

Aodh did not move, his perpetually smirking mouth now a full on snarl, twin sets of canine fully exposed as his fist seemed to shake as it gripped the knife, raw power ready to be released. "You heard that thrall's geise, brother, as *Tiarna* I will act if you are too cowardly to do so".

Fiachra let out a low growl and Alix's breath caught as Fiachra's back seemed to ripple, his muscles seeming to swell as if activated.

"It is a geise, brother. It cannot be changed". He said, voice still quiet but resonating with violence. Alix had not seen such anger from the Fae before, it shocked her, scared her. And yet, there was something else there too. He was, protecting her, this beast who had carried her back here now standing sentinel, watching over her. *But,* Alix thought, *why?*

Aodh laughed a bitter laugh. "Maybe so, brother, yet it is a thrall. Its life is meaningless". Alix's blood chilled at his words, as her breath seemed to quicken. He was right, her life was not her own, if Aodh wanted too he could just take it, or worse. She would never have her freedom again. The point

Bevan had so well illustrated, crashing home with Aodh's words.

She did not hear Fiachra's response, instead, she sank to a crouch, hugging her knees to her chest as she felt the truth of her situation finally settle on her, in her. The knowledge that she was no different than the beasts to these Fae. A pig fattened for slaughter, unaware of the coming feast.

She did not cry, she did not have any tears left to give, instead she just stayed there staring into the dirt of the floor, her pen, her slaughterhouse. There were no words available to her anymore, unfair, evil, cruel. Those did not explain this, it could not. Was it cruel for the chicken to be butchered?

"No", came the rumble from Fiachra, "Her life, is not yours to take". Alix's eyes rose slowly to look at him. The quiet voice seemingly mismatched to the tall powerful frame that promised a brutal and painful death to any who opposed him.

"She is mine, brother, and under my protection". Aodh seemed shocked for a moment at Fiachra's announcement before turning to her warriors with a laugh. "The second brother forgets himself, my *Fianna*, he believes that because he is *my* brother, he is somehow *my* equal." Aodh chuckled, "Filthy mutt, you are second only for the humour it allows me to watch Brigit suffer. You are nothing. In fact, my *Fianna*, remind him". The rabid, red-eyed Fae snarled in anticipation, flashes of light, as knives leaving sheathes caught the light from the moon. Fiachra did not draw his own, but instead hunkered lower, arms spread wide.

With a howl the warriors moved, swarming forward a river of crazed foxes with a rabbit in the sights. The first to reach *Fianna* pounced forward silver knife held over their head, ready to bring in a downward stroke into Fiachra's head.

Fiachra's left arm flashed forward, his thick fist closing around the *Fianna's* neck as the Fae lord closed his fist, red blooming between his fingers as the leaping Fae crumbled.

Fiachra caught the next one by the head, slamming him into the ground as his head seemed to collapse into shattered bones and gore from the impact. The next two warriors to reach the Fae Lord found their mark, however, silver blades rising and falling as they quickly stabbed the taller Fae over and over. Fiachra roared as he threw them off, throwing them with force at their charging compatriots, sending them sprawling across the ground, limbs bent and broken from the impact.

With an explosive howl, Fiachra ripped the stump from where he had been sitting out of the earth, raising it over his head as he bellowed. "Hold!" came a voice like ice and the giant paused, stump still raised above his head, aimed at his brother. With a snarl one of the red-eyed fae stepped forward, driving his knife hilt deep into Fiachra's midriff. Alix gave a screech, thankfully muffled by her hands as she held them over her lips.Fiachra stumbled to one knee, blood beginning to stream   freely   from   the   wound.

"Hold! Damn you! I will have your eyes for breakfast, hold!" Alix turned and spotted the owner of the voice, as Brigit came running down the path from the palace, several of her own *Fianna* in tow. Aodh snarled and rolled his eyes as his sister came to a stop in front of him.

"You may lead brother, but did you think you could hide this from me?" she snarled back as Aodh took a few steps back eyes dark and reflective as he paced back and forth, fingered the knife at his waist.

"Shut it Brigit, this is decided. The thrall dies". He turned back to his *Fianna*, and nodded, Brigit stepped towards

Aodh and raised sharp nails to his neck. The fierce Fae stiffened as his sister's claws bit into his skin drawing blood.

"Nothing is decided until I have said so" she hissed at her brother, her *Fianna* drawing their knives as they squared off against Aodh's. The two groups of Fae snarled at each other before Aodh, flinching as Brigit drove her nails in deeper, conceded with a bark. "Fine! Damn you, we will discuss this at court". Only then did she withdraw her nails, wiping the blood from them on her brother's tattooed chest before turning to Fiachra,

"Oh do put that down, brother," smirking at the tree stump he still held overhead, "Aodh won't break your toys today". She finished before stalking back to the palace. "Oh and since neither of you have noticed, the thrall has been watching you two as you measured cocks". She added as her warriors fell in behind her, following the slinking Fae as she sauntered back to the palace, laughing sensuously as she went. Fiachra, dropping the stump and gripping the hilt still protruding from his stomach, turned as he and Aodh stared as one, finding her crouched in the barracks door frame.

She had a momentary urge to run, to escape their angry stares as dozens of eyes turned on her, shining in the moonlight in the unique and unsettling way that predator's eyes do. Instead, she slowly stood, hands smoothing the blanket she wore wrapped around her. Despite being several times thicker than the dress she was forced to wear, she felt more naked before the Fae than she had ever felt, unable to meet their eyes as she continuously adjusted the blanket.

Aodh let out another bitter laugh. "Brother, you protect this? Many woman of quality and high birth toss themselves at your feet. Ha! Educate your jade, fool, she seems to have forgotten her station". Aodh's *Fianna* took up his laugh as they retreated, wounded Fae carried on their backs, leaving the still-hunched Fiachra to his wounds. Alix and Fiachra stared at each other a moment before Fiachra, attempting to rise, gasped and fell back to his knees. Alix felt herself yearning to run to him, surprise following at the strength of the emotion, before she cautiously stepped out of the barracks and, once out into the open air, moved to Fiachra's side.

He was covered in wounds, some deep and bleeding freely. Though none looked as bad as the one he gripped, the hilt of the knife seemed to sprout from his decorated skin. "What do I do?" she asked, voice surprisingly level. She was unsure whether removing the knife would help or hinder. "You are very brave", Fiachra said instead. "Most humans know to stay inside when they hear our roars". He chuckled at his own joke before grimacing at the pain. Alix ignored the Fae and repeated her question. He ignored her in turn and said "I owe you an explanation", he paused. "It is not fair you do not know your geise".

Alix decided for him and quickly pulled the knife from the Fae. He roared and being so close to the Fae, Alix tried to scamper back, to flee the wounded beast lest it kill her in his anger, but his hand reached out gripping her hand, not painfully, but firmly. She did not move, though she felt sure if she had tried he would have let go. Instead, she held his hand in hers and squeezed back.

Fiachra lay back on the ground and his breathing relaxed, coming less ragged as he chuckled painfully to himself, "I avoid violence ten years just to get stabbed in my own home". He chuckled again, stiffening as the pain bit. He did not release her hand either. "What did Bevan see?" Alix asked, her question cut his laughter short.

"Your geise, your future". He said simply. "And it appears what she saw was important enough to tell almost everyone". He sighed. "I can tell you, but your geise is supposed to be your own. Unknown to others but yourself, Bevan did a forbidden thing telling me, telling Aodh". He grimaced as he pushed himself up resting against the now upturned stump. "It is not my place to tell it to you Alix, I should not even know it, I apologise for knowing it. It is disrespectful to you to do so. Bevan must tell you". Alix was about to push him again, the sense that he would tell her if she persisted lingered for a moment but yet another wince from Fiachra stayed her tongue.

"You need bandages and stitches" she said, "honestly, if you were human I would say you would be dead". He nodded his agreement. "I will send for some. Please, if you can fetch some assistance to get me back to my room, I will be further in your debt". His breathing, though stronger, still came in ragged bursts. Alix rose then, Fiachra's hand letting go as soon as she tried to pull it away, she ran back to the barracks, expecting to have to wake up Aine, and ask the older woman what to do, but instead, she found a welcoming party of dozens of thralls waiting, obviously listening as the two had talked.

Alix opened her mouth to speak but Aine cut her off, "Yes yes girl, you and you," she said, spinning to select two of the largest strongest men, "go carry the Lord Fiachra to his chambers. "Maeve, busy yourself with grabbing bandages and go grab a healer", Aine spun to Alix now. "And you, child, are supposed to be resting. I understand you are in a bit of a sorry state but a warning to you, never leave this building again without your collar." Alix's hands shot to her neck, feeling her bare skin, "oh", was all she managed as the thralls began to do their tasks around her. Aine smiled softly, "back to bed, girl, get your rest". She moved to continue her barking orders and Alix returned to her now empty room. She lay in bed but sleep didn't come and she lay awake staring at the ceiling, the events of the night replaying in her head.

Chapter 9

Alix shuffled uncomfortably from her seat as Fiachra fussed with the mess of scrolls that made up the ever-messy main room of Fiachra's apartments. The large Fae had spoken only once since pointed her to the chair with a silent command to wait. Alix, having just witnessed the fury of this Fae male in action, plopped down onto the fur pillow without complaint.

"I am sorry for the state of my room", he apologised, and Alix was shocked to hear the truth in his words. It took her slightly aback. After all, he had seemed to have no issue with parading around in little more than a loin cloth while she slaved away with cleaning and washing all his clothes and bedding, but Alix did not feel like now was the right time to raise that fact and instead, blinking, said "okay".

Fiachra noticed the discomfort in her voice, however, and looked up to her. Again, those green eyes seemed to pierce her, her breath catching slightly as she felt her skin prickly under his gaze. He searched her eyes, his own dropping almost too quickly to notice to her lips before he pulled them away.

"I… I am sorry you had to see that, Alix, you are owed an explanation". Fiachra ran his hand through his rain-wet hair, and Alix attempted not to notice the way his shirtless chest, still dripping from his sentinel post in the rain, caught the candlelight as he moved, each muscle tensed from the stress of the days events.

She coughed as she dropped her eyes to her hands and began to fidget with her fingers. "I just want to know… what is wrong". She said. "You say my geise is my future, what does that mean? And why suddenly does everyone want to kill me?" She was shocked, and the fear in her voice, the anxiety and dread that was always there but kept at arm's length, started to creep back in.

Fiachra was there in an instant, and he knelt in front of her, his large green eyes looking up into hers. "No one will hurt you, Alix, I won't allow that". She was shocked at the growl in his voice. It seemed so feral, so vicious. As if the hidden beast that lay within was poking through, a reminder of just who he was. What he was. Alix swallowed involuntarily as his hands, now gripping her thigh, squeezed, reminding her of the strength of those arms, those tattooed shoulders, still glistening. She nodded briskly and pulled ever so slightly from his grip, and he let her, all pressure disappeared as soon as she made any move to pull away.

The Fae lord coloured slightly as if he had just realised how close he had been to her, where his hand had been placed so closely too. "Let me fetch you water", he stumbled as he turned to grab two copper cups and a large pitcher of water, he poured her one, then himself, then returned to the pillow on the floor, blessedly further from her than when he had been kneeling between her knees.

"You promised me answers once before," Alix blurted out, speaking before the Fae lord lowered his cup from his luscious lips. "Why would I believe this time is different?" She asked. Fiachra placed his cup before him, and he looked at her then, and Alix almost regretted the question at the awaiting heat in his eyes.

"I told you before that this... enslavement is my people's way. But it is not my way. I truly did mean to answer your questions however, I was warned, the eternal politics of my people are ever at play". He paused, sighing as his massive frame seemed to shrink in on itself, those green eyes showing something new, sorrow.

"There is no love lost between my siblings and I. We are all our father's children, but my mother, she was our father's first wife. I am cursed by her breed". He said with no hint of malice. A tree complaining of the storm, to be weathered and endured but never overcome.

"Your mother?" Alix asked gently but curious, she had not yet been able to discern age between most of the Fae, their Fox-like faces and strong bodies sitting on the cusp of being human yet, somehow, ageless. She wondered what Fae woman within these walls could have borne such a male.

"She died while I was very young". Fiachra said, his voice quiet. "It is a story I do not wish to tell, but I will if you ask it of me. The essential piece of it is she was a Highland Fae, A Neamhaí. She was not supposed to have me, my father was displeased, and as punishment for being from inferior stock, I will always sit last among his heirs."

Alix nodded in understanding, and though a part of her wanted to push, to understand more of this giant male and what made him tick, she had more pressing issues in mind. "What is my geise, and why are people trying to kill me?" She repeated instead. Fiachra was silent a moment before he began. "A geise is your life, your future and all future possibilities, the essential story of your life, your moment of glory or anguish, your greatest moment or your final ones. For each person, it is different, but all living creatures have one, a true vision of what is to be in your life, an unavoidable moment that will define you individually and in time. It is a gift of life that all beings possess. My sister has the sight, she can read them and... well, she read yours".

She steeled herself back, straightening, and she was proud at how little her voice shook as she asked. "What is my geise?". Fiachra was silent a long moment, toying with the cup in front of him before answering.

"Alix, you will destroy us all". He said simply. The silence stretched for a long moment before Alix let out a snort of laughter. Instantly, her hands clamped over her mouth as Fiachra, shock evident on his way, looked up wide-eyed at the young woman across from him. The other confusion on his face allowed a second snort to escape, and before she knew what she was doing, laughter had won over, and she laughed and chortled at the ridiculousness of her life. Fiachra watched concern in his eyes before an involuntary twitch at his lips had him covering his mouth, asking if she was okay. Alix, now on her back and giddy with laughter, caught his eyes, and they seemed to soften, that dark green seeming to melt as they looked at her, and a hideous laugh escaped his lips. It caught her so off guard her laughing ceased for a moment before continuing as the Fae lord tried his best to stifle his booming awful laughter behind giant hands. They laughed themselves, exhausted, both lying now on the carpeted floor as reality and sobriety started to creep back into their senses.

"This is just awful", Alix moaned, rubbing at the now puffy red eyes. Fiachra grunted his approval before pushing himself up, Alix was suddenly aware of his body beside her and slowly moved from him, pushing herself up to face him. She pretended not to notice the hand that hesitated to touch her, fingers retreating at the last possible moment. "What now?" She asked once they were both settled back onto their cushions, the space between them again back to a respectable distance, a lord and his thrall. "Well, I guess now you get to ask me more questions". He said. So she did.

Alix asked her questions, and they stayed up long into the night.

Chapter 10

The next morning, Fiachra led Alix through the gardens of the estate, pointedly ignoring the stares of the passing Fae. It had been a week since that night in the rain, and though none of the Fae had attempted to approach her, clearly the truth of her geise had gotten out, and most Fae now viewed her with outright disgust. Her friends, of course, had been quick to ask the many thralls, normally quiet, letting any and all questions loose as soon as they were alone within their barracks.

Fiachra had been true to his word and had not left her side since that night, holding his nightly vigil on the lonely stump, now awkwardly protruding from the ground, outside the barracks door as soon as she returned after chores. It was odd having him at her back all day, especially since she spent so much of the day on all floors scrubbing and sweeping what was supposedly his home.

She had given up trying to ask for space, her originally timid attempts quickly getting more and more brazen before Fiachra shut down any attempt at making him leave her alone. "I promised you I would keep you safe", he had said. "I am not going anywhere". Alix rolled her eyes at the male, quietly in awe at how stupid male pride seemed to be universal across species, but if he refused to leave, fine, Alix would just take him up on his other promise then.

"How old are you?" She asked as Fiachra was bent over, inspecting an ailing bush that was distinctly yellow against its peers. Fiachra did not look so shocked this time, well used by now to the oftentimes personal and off-topic questions Alix had been throwing his way the past several days.

"By your count? Probably a hundred and fifteen, or is it twenty years? My people would say I am still in my early adult years". Alix wasn't shocked to hear the age of the Fae lord. All the fae were old compared to humans, that was not a secret that was hidden. It was, however, surprising given the gap in ages between him and his siblings.

"Wait, you are almost twice as old as Aodh? And what forty years older than Brigid?" She asked, curiosity pulling at her. Fiachra smiled as he rose to turn to her, and she blushed as his green eyes seemed to sparkle in the mid-day light.

"Thirty-seven years, actually, I remember when she was born, I was so bitter at first, I saw her as a challenger when she was born... my father was clear on my place in the family by then. She and any other children to come were to usurp me, take what I was beginning to see as mine by right. But then I saw her for the first time.

"She was tiny, and Father was so protective of her, they knew she would be a seer from birth. Father was so proud. I snuck into her nursery one night. I don't know what I intended to do. I felt it only right to take her away from him after my mother. But she just looked up at me and smiled. It was then I truly realised what made me different from my father". He smiled sorrowfully and brushed the dirt from his hands as he began to walk further down the garden path.

"But they hate you," Alix offered, and she regretted it as soon as she saw the pain in his eyes, the hurt.

"Yes, but only because they were raised too. To see each of us as a threat. Our alliance is an uneasy one, but it has held for decades. It will hold a few decades more". Alix walked in silence beside him for a long moment, Fiachra was lost to his memories as Alix tried to form a complete picture from all he was telling her.

"Alliance?" She asked, promoting the Fae lord to continue. "Our father ruled here, and he was a powerful Tiarna, they said in his prime he came to this valley and killed the previous court with his bare hands, they said the valley ran red with blood that night. By the morning, all the *Fianna* had sworn to him, those that didn't found their flayed bodies crucified on the peaks. Their death screams haunt this valley to this very day. That was centuries ago.

"I was his firstborn to a concubine of the former lord. As such, he expected me to succeed him eventually. At least, that was what my mother said was his plan originally. The only issue is we have much longer lifespans than you, and well... based on how he took power, he worried about me, my mother... he eventually found a new concubine of local stock and breed more acceptable to produce heirs and from her came Brigid, Aodh and Kadir. My father loved them as he loved anything, imagined pawns to do his bidding.

"He ranked us then, constantly adjusting and moving us in his order of favourites. Constantly competing for the attention, the power he offered. Yet, it never came. My people live a long while, Alix. How long do you think it took for us to realise he never meant to share that power? Maybe it is just my age, but I discovered that truth first". He paused then, the pair now stopped at a turn in the cobble path, a beautiful vista of the birch-filled valley welcoming them to rest awhile, to the beauty of nature seeming to try and distract from the words now tumbling from the Fae's mouth.

"We are all skilled, Aodh commands the *Fianna*, and I truly think no one could capture their loyalty better. They crave a master, a ruthless leader, something I could never be. Brigid, well, she is the spiritual leader of so many of my people, her place is unquestionably in the court. Kadir was young. Still, he had yet to finish his training with the *Fianna* then, still spending his days in the pits covered in mud and shit fighting those other feral younglings. I had to prove my worth. My father recognised my strength, my speed. I may not be able to command armies, but I can destroy them". He paused for a moment, his mind seemingly caught in a past memory, before looking at her. The roses on his forearms seemed to dance as he fidgeted with his fingers, seemingly at war with himself to reveal his past.

"I killed people, Alix. A lot of people. More than you can probably guess and in ways I hope you could never fathom. I hated myself for it, hated him for making me feel like I had to. I hated him more when he began to have each one tattooed on me". He looked down at himself now at the thick vines and flowers that obscured the ink of old tattoos that were evident underneath.

"Every morning as I awoke, saw myself in the mirror… it was a reminder of the lives I ended, of how I ended them. Something had to change". He took in a massive breath then, inhaling the air as it came up the valley, cool and delightful as it pulled at his pants, at her robe. Alix wondered then if his Fae senses allowed him to smell more on the air and see more in the colours that the forest threw back at them in hues of red and yellows. She added it to her mental list of unasked questions.

"What happened then?" She prompted, hoping the Fae, his ever-shining green eyes now seeming distant, dark.

"We decided then we would kill him, take his place and rule as a court, Aodh as our leader, as first brother, Kadir his heir and me finally left alone. Though they were all afraid of my father, of his power, I volunteered to do the deed. In exchange for my own true freedom, no killing, no torturing. Peace for as long as I had left to live. Only for that would I do this, and they agreed".

They stood in silence for a moment, Alix felt torn, wanting to offer comfort to the male, even as her body screamed out at the danger of him and of allowing herself to get close to him, her owner.

Instead, she trusts her chin in the direction of a slow moving caravan of people. "Where are they going?" She asked. He turned and smirked at her.
"Let's go find out,". He said before starting down the cobble path at a pace that almost had Alix running to keep up.

The caravan strode lazily along the path, and by the time the pair had caught up to them, they had turned off the road and were beginning to unload their burden, passing large baskets filled with red fruit, large and succulent, to waiting thralls who took the baskets before retreating into the compound nestled between the road and flowing brook behind.

Fiachra approached the large Fae female leading the group and was annoyed at the jealousy that sprung up as the female hungrily looked over Fiachra, eyes taking full advantage of the sheer loose-fitting fabric of his trousers. Fiachra did not seem to notice and instead inquired about the load they carried. It turned out that they carried colorful fruits from the far orchards. The harvest was good this year, and there would be plenty of stout drink soon, she beamed. As soon as the thralls had finished the juicing and fermenting necessary, she added fiercely, prompting all those humans within hearing to quicken their step. She finished with an offer to sample some of their offerings privately, but Fiachra politely declined.

Chapter 11

When they returned to his quarters, Fiachra closed the heavy door behind him, tossing off his shirt as it had grown damp from the heat. She nervously retreated to his bed, finding herself oddly comfortable with making herself at home here. From her view, she could see the muscles along his back tight with tension. The ink running down his spine seemed to ripple as he pushed himself back and turned towards her. She allowed herself to run her eyes down his body and suppressed a shiver at the sight of him.

His broad shoulders were decorated so beautifully with dark ink renditions of the life he had lived. She followed the string of holly leaves down his chest as it met and merged with tightly woven threads of ink that wove two ravens sitting low on his stomach, drawing her eyes further down towards the thin saffron trousers and the thick bulge that hid the length she had seen the wagon driver eying earlier.

After the caravan and sampling some of the local goods, Fiachra had taken her out to the forests and shown her the long woods and large homes the Fae had on the ridge overlooking the lake. It didn't have a name Fiachra had told her, which was odd, she thought, since the Fae seemed keen on giving unnecessary titles at every opportunity they got.

She grew tired from the days activities and leaned lazily back into the plump pillows. Reflecting, she thought about how she and this Fae had grown close over these last few days. The odd comfort she felt in his presence left her unsettled, and she felt a pang of guilt as she thought of the hardships her clann members must be enduring.

She could not let herself grow complicit. She must act, must plan her escape. No matter how kind this Fae appeared to be, he was still the enemy, and she must fight to protect her friends and her found family. She gulped as his eyes met hers, and he seemed as lost as she was in this moment.

Scheming, she improvised a plan. She thought of the thrall and all the ways they could serve their masters, wondering if hers would be interested in similar comforts. She would get close to him, earn his trust, and use it to find a window of opportunity. Her captor was a man of few weaknesses, but she thought she had found one, and she would not allow it to slip away. If she happened to benefit physically from any encounter, it was just a happy accident, or so she told herself.

She rearranged her clothes, plucking at the thin blouse as if at a loose thread before pulling her legs back to her chest, allowing the already short tunic to slide further up her thighs. *An inch more,* she thought, *and Keemre would have had me breaking rocks for a week.* But desperate times called for desperate solutions.

"What is it you wish from me, my lord?" she said, carefully trailing her eyes up his body, letting her voice drip with sensuality. She looked up into his eyes and, after a flash of surprise, she saw a quiet fire growing there. Alix calmed her face, not allowing her shock and excitement at the effect she was having to show. She was playing a part, she told herself, allowing herself to act the role he wished of her. To be the innocent thrall who had been seduced by the gentle master. A part of her noted the whisper of truth in that but decided not to think about it much deeper.

Fiachra stood now at the edge of the bed. He still did not speak, and, again, Alix shuddered at the sight of him, his shoulders rose and fell in line with his breathing, the tight mounds of muscles seeming to pulse with the motion. Gods, she needed to be calm, she was in control here, and he would not intimidate her. She pulled herself to the edge of the bed and sat before him. She took a moment to study the bulge between his legs, now mere inches away. She took her time admiring it and made sure he knew she was looking. Up close, the fabric was almost as sheer as her own, and she smiled as she noticed the tightening of the fabric.

She looked up to him then, just like she had seen those devoted ones did when their favourite came by to visit the barracks, through her lashes, her eyes big, trusting, asking him wordlessly what she should do next. She suppressed the sense of satisfaction she felt as she saw the desperation, the hungry need within those eyes of uncountable green. Somehow she had him snared. Whatever odd energy she felt between them, she knew he felt it too. She took a breath as she reminded herself that she must remain vigilant, purposeful. The ache growing between her legs was just an unfortunate side-effect of nature, not a sign of affection towards her captor.

In a flash, his eyes turned so dark they appeared black. His demeanour changing in seconds. "Never attempt this again". The words were said with such quiet rage that, for a moment, Alix felt she must have misheard.

"What?" she said, But Fiachra turned from her, resting his hands on the ledge of the large window overlooking the valley. "I thought this is what you wanted". She said, suddenly feeling awkward and ashamed. Fiachra did not speak, but she could see his muscles writhe as he kept his face from her. Had she misread his need? Why did his rejection sting this badly?

"I cannot, Alix," He said, "Please, go". For a moment, she almost did, sitting there feeling like a chastised child. Suddenly rage built within her, knowing she had failed her clann once again, feeling the pain of confusion at the swirl of emotions in her heart, she allowed herself to shatter.

"You and your kind stole me from my home, your brother killed my family, and in between all this suffering and hell, I try to find moments of joy. Something to provide some pleasure and distraction from my drastically changed life and you, you, you…. You do this?" She was screaming now, but she no longer cared. A seal had been broken, the words were coming whether she wanted them to or not.

"Why?! I don't want to be here! I don't want to feel things for you. But why can't you just let me find some meaningless joy in this life." She let in a sharp gasp at her unexpected declaration, hoping he would not focus on it. Decidedly pushing it to the back of her mind, attributing the words to stress and overwhelm from all she had endured.

Fiachra's head dropped then, and he turned. He said something under his breath so softly that Alix could not hear it. "What?" she asked hesitantly, suddenly aware of how far she had overstepped. Fiachra sighed, and his green eyes rose to meet hers. "It is not meaningless to me, Alix. I… I believe I may be starting to enjoy your company more than is appropriate. It may be best if-

"If what?" Alix interrupted, crossing from the bed to stand firm before the giant Fae, "Best if you send me back to the fields? I am just a thrall after all, right? Easy to use, easy to replace. Maybe you will find another thrall better suited to your preferences". She moved towards the door and stopped as Fiachra gently placed his hand on her shoulder. He kept it there a moment, waiting, she thought, to see what she would do. She leaned into him ever so slightly, and suddenly, both of his arms were wrapping her up from behind.

"Please don't go". He said to her back, "I care for you, Alix, I am starting to look forward to the mornings when I can see your face again. I… I am not good at this, Alix, but I care for you, and I want to help you, you and your clann. I mean it, I just". He sighed and ran his large tattooed hands through his hair. "I just don't want to promise you something I cannot do. I have killed people, Alix, and it has changed me. I hate that you and your family are enslaved, but I cannot grip a knife again, Alix, I can't". She was shocked at his admission, his voice was as close to frantic as she had ever heard a Fae be by the end and Alix quickly found herself shushing and rubbing tears from Fiachra's eyes as he spoke. Had he known her intentions all this time? To use him to free her clann?

"It's okay, then let's just go slow, okay?" she found herself saying, for some reason not giving in despite him somehow seeing through her ruse. *Is this really a ruse, though?* She pushed the thought to the back of her mind as he tried to move from her again, but she pushed firmly, and he gave in, allowing her to push him down to the mattress.

"Please", she begged, staring down at him, still holding his hands to the mattress, her short shift had ridden up her thighs, and the soft touch of his skin against her inner thighs sent tingles through her.

"Please," she repeated again, seeing the rejection begin to rise again in his eyes, the fear, the hunger. "You are not like them, Fiachra, I want you". She said, surprised at the desperation in her voice. "Every part of you", she continued as she slowly started to move her hips up and down, allowing her wetness to graze his cock through the thin fabric of his trousers. He growled then, eyes flashing a warning as he began to sit up gently, attempting to remove her from his lap.

She pushed back and was surprised, yet again, when he let her. Slight shock in his own eyes as Alix bent over him to stare into those grass green eyes, those eyes that had seen so much, had seen her, and at just this moment, she was worried they would swallow her up and drown her in their depths.

"I. Want. You". She repeated. "I... *need* you", she whispered. She had meant for the words to be reassuring, alluring even, and Alix made a conscious choice to ignore how deeply desperate she sounded. How horrifyingly true the words felt in that moment, even though she barely knew this Fae. What the fuck was she doing.

Instead, she focused on those eyes. How his pupils widened when he looked at her, the hunger and no small amount of desperation of his own shining through. She began to move her hips again, starting at the tip of his now growing cock, and as far down as she could, before starting the process again. He met her lunge for lunge, the cool fabric of his trousers now wet with her, his cock bulging through, pleading to be freed.

She leaned over him, and she took in the pleasure, the desire. *Fuck*, she loved how he looked at her. His hands twitched, a small plea to allow them to wander, but she held him there, throwing her head back and letting him watch her as she ground into his hips, rubbing that sensitive bundle of nerves over the broad head of his tip over and over, not bothering to hold back her voice as moans of pleasure began to creep from her lips.

As she writhed, she watched his restraint collapse entirely. A growl of need releasing him from his seemingly virtuous intentions. "Fuck". He said. The word escaping his gritted teeth as, with each stroke, he bucked his hips in increasingly more desperate attempts. Alix giggled at the sight. The great giant of the *Aos Sí* reduced to a male, his desperation for her exciting her, giving her a sense of confidence that had her dip her head, lips meeting lips as his mouth opened to her, taking in her tongue, kissing her deeply. She released his hands, and they jumped into action, one grabbing her ass, guiding her back and forth as she continued to grind hard enough that she hoped it might rip through the fabric, allowing him into her fully. The other hand went to her head, wrapping his long, thick fingers through her curly, auburn hair as he pulled her closer to him, tongue exploring her mouth between moans. He pulled away from the kiss, and Alix was about to explode at his leaving before he moved to her neck, kissing and biting her neck, punctuating each one with a quiet "fuck" against her ear as she continued her movement.

Their movements became more frantic as their hips met over and over, finally, with all sense of sense lost, Alix allowed Fiachra to take her fully, flipping her onto the bed as she opened her legs wide, pulling him in. Their mouths met again with a fury Alix had never known possible, Fiachra began to trust hungrily, violently into her. "Yes", she said, "more," and Fiachra obliged. She pulled his mouth back to her neck, and she moaned desperately while Fiachra continued his hard and fast pace. She could feel something growing within her, and she sank her nails into Fiachra's biceps as she opened her mouth to plead, "Yes, I am so close, please, yes!" she felt her toes begin to tingle that familiar warm feeling filling her mind. She let her head roll back as Fiachra continued his thrusts. "I don't know how much longer I can keep going," Fiachra said, each syllable punctuated by a loud strike of his hips meeting hers.

"I'm coming" was all Alix was able to manage. Fiachra's shocked chuckle filled her ears. He said, "Good girl", and then, with renewed vigour, thrust a final few times, Alix was stunned at his sudden boldness, pulling him in, nails carving grooves in his tattooed back as the two lay there, exhausted.

"That was…", Alix paused, at a loss for words from under the weight of the Fae, still trying to catch his breath. "The best sex you've ever had?", Fiachra joked nervously. They laughed together, Fiachra reaching up to stroke lost auburn curls from Alix's forehead.

"Eh, I don't know about the best ever, but it certainly was loud!" came a third voice before Alix had time to even reconcile the fact there was a third voice. Fiachra had already moved to stand between her and the unannounced visitor. Brigit stood in the doorframe cutting slices from an apple with that long hideous knife as she stood smiling at the two of them.

"Oh Fiachra, you make it too easy sometimes". She said, "It is almost too cruel sometimes with you." Fiachra stared his sister down in nothing but his loincloth. "Leave Brigit, now". She chuckled at his tone but spun on her heel and left. "Too easy!" she called behind her, "You make this too easy!"

To be Continued...

End of Part One.

Made in United States
Troutdale, OR
02/24/2025

29272283R00077